Keep It In The Family

Patsy Collins

In memory of my Aunty Barbara.
We lost you far too soon.

Contents

1. Dizzy

Dennis answered his mobile. "Yes, love?"

"Dad, I think I've started. I'm fine… but I'd like you to come if you can."

"Of course I can." He'd said he'd be there, so he'd be there. Dennis, unlike some he could name, wasn't the sort to let his darling Melanie give birth all alone. Dizzy! Even the man's name sounded unreliable. Well, Dizzy had a very important photo shoot two weeks before his first child was due and had gone swanning off to the Outer Hebrides. Honestly, you couldn't make it up.

The boy didn't take any notice of Dennis's opinion, just told him to 'Chill'. Dennis did just that and as a result, they always gave each other a fairly frosty reception.

Dennis had cancelled all his appointments for the weeks before and after the expected birth, just to make sure he'd be available, should he be needed. He collected a bag he'd packed ready, locked up put a note through his neighbour's door and drove to Melanie's home.

"How are you doing, love?" he asked as he let himself in. Melanie must have seen him coming, because she was already in the hallway.

"Absolutely fine. It's just like they said it would be in the classes. I've rung the midwife to let her know. She was in the area so she popped in to check my blood pressure. It's fine and I told her you were on the way, so I can stay here and ring her back when the contractions are more frequent."

"And Dizzy? Is he on his way?"

"No, Dad." She put up a hand to stop the outburst she must have guessed was coming. "I haven't contacted him."

"Why on earth not?"

"I don't think he'll be able to get back in time and I don't want him missing the shoot for nothing."

"Nothing? Can't get back? He should never have gone, not when you could go into labour any minute."

"He didn't know about that, Dad. I didn't tell him about the high blood pressure and all the rest of it. I didn't want to worry him or make him miss this shoot. He had to go now because the seals are only there, giving birth, for a short time."

Dennis didn't see why Dizzy had been let off the worrying, when he and his daughter had been so concerned about the baby, but he kept that to himself.

"And I didn't want him to be able to let me down," Melanie whispered.

Dizzy did that. He was always turning up late, forgetting to do things, or making silly mistakes. He wouldn't be there for the birth of his baby, but this time it wouldn't be his fault, so she wouldn't hold it against him.

Dennis offered to make tea. In the kitchen, he made a couple of calls; first to let the bowls club know he might not be in the following day because of the baby and then he contacted a few other people he thought should know.

They drank their tea and chatted between Melanie's contractions. She laughed at him writing down the times.

"I like to be organised," he told her.

"So does Dizzy really. He's just not always good at it. I

was slightly surprised when he phoned on Wednesday to say he was on the Island taking pictures of the seal pups. I was sure he'd have forgotten a camera, or missed one of the ferries or a train or something."

"Train?" Dennis had imagined his son-in-law had flown up; probably in club class.

"Up to Waterloo, the tube, then a sleeper into Scotland."

"And more than one ferry?"

"It's a very remote location. He got a ferry to Barra, then he had to go over on this tiny little boat and it only runs a couple of times a day, so I thought he'd miss a connection somewhere. So you see, he really can't possibly get back in time."

"I'm afraid you're right."

Dennis gave Melanie a hug, because it looked like she was going to cry.

"You'll be a brilliant granddad, just like you were a great father, still are. You never missed a birthday or school play, even when Mum was ill and you were looking after both of us as well as working."

"I'm sure your Dizzy will be a good father in his own way," Dennis reassured her. He knew his daughter so well, he'd guessed that's what was on her mind.

"Will he?"

"Of course. Oh, I know he's been late a few times and sometimes forgets he's promised to pick up the shopping on the way home from a job ..."

"More than a few times." Melanie said just what he was thinking himself.

"He's always been there for the important things though, hasn't he? He was in the church before you on your wedding day."

Melanie didn't know about the text Dennis received in the car on the way asking him to make sure the driver went as slowly as possible. It was only Dennis who'd spotted Dizzy and the best man running through the lychgate as he helped his daughter from the car and adjusted her veil.

"Yes, I suppose, and usually there's a good reason for him being late or forgetting things."

Dennis nodded. Dizzy apologised at the reception and explained the car they were supposed to travel in had broken down and he and the best man had run three miles, not just up the church path. He'd been late home on his and Melanie's first wedding anniversary because he'd ordered her a bouquet just like the one she'd carried at her wedding and put on her mother's grave. The florist accidentally sent the flowers to the wrong place and it had taken Dizzy two hours to track them down. Really, he wasn't such a bad man. He loved Melanie and would love Dennis's grandchild too. That's what was really important.

Melanie's contractions became stronger and more frequent and, on the midwife's advice, Dennis drove her to hospital. He took the bag she'd packed herself and put it in the boot next to the one he'd packed in case she was away from home when she'd started labour.

It was more than six hours after he'd received her call that Dennis finally got his daughter settled into the hospital ward. They were told to expect a wait of several more hours.

"Nothing to worry about, first babies often take a while," Dennis was assured when he made enquiries.

"Don't fuss, Dad," Melanie said. "It's bad enough with the staff checking my blood pressure and everything all the time. You just sit there and keep me calm."

Dennis tried during the next few hours. He joked about her childhood and told her what he could remember about her own birth. He didn't like to say he hadn't known much about it because as soon as things started in earnest, he'd passed out and spent the rest of the time sat with his head between his knees. That was a long time ago though. He was almost certain he'd cope better this time.

"Sit down, Dad."

He hadn't even realised he'd been pacing around the room. He sat and held Melanie's hand as another terrifying contraction gripped her. If she'd let go he'd have gone in search of someone to give her gas and air.

"Remember to breathe," he said at intervals. He was advising himself as much as instructing his daughter.

"I'm so honoured you wanted me at the birth of my first grandchild," he said. He wasn't sure she heard because she was yelling and digging her nails into his hand again.

"I knew you'd be here, Dad. You've never let me down."

He wondered if his son-in-law's name had been chosen in the maternity ward, because he was feeling dizzy himself. Thankfully the midwife arrived just then and he was able to focus on her confident face, not his daughter's sweaty one.

"Things seem to be moving along nicely now," she said as Melanie yelled again.

Dennis put his head between his knees. He breathed. More people came into the room, but they were tending to Melanie not him; just as they should be. During what seemed to be a lull in the proceedings, someone squeezed his shoulder. Dennis pulled himself up straight and tried to look confident. He didn't want anyone worrying about him.

"OK, Dad?" It was Dizzy.

"Yes, yes fine. What are you …?" He couldn't finish the query though, because Melanie was now being urged to push.

A few minutes later, the room was filled with the sound of a baby crying. Dennis had forgotten how much noise could come from such a tiny person. After a few checks, Melanie and her family were left alone. Dizzy held his new son on his lap and wrapped an arm protectively round him as he explained how he'd got there.

"I'd just finished the shoot when I felt my phone vibrate. I guessed what the message said, so shouted to the rest that they'd have to finish off and pack up while I was reading it." Dizzy lifted the baby to his face and nuzzled the child's neck. "I got back across the island in less than half the time it took to get out and persuaded the guy on the first ferry to take me over even though it wasn't the right time. On the way I explained what the hurry was and he got onto his radio and soon found a lorry driver who was coming down this way. The driver picked me up from the second ferry. I'd have missed that if the first ferryman, crikey …" Dizzy broke off to run a hand through his hair. "I don't even know his name, hadn't got onto his radio and persuaded it to wait for me. Those Island people are just so friendly and helpful."

He pulled back the blue blanket covering his son and counted each tiny, yet chubby, finger and toe. "The lorry driver brought me the whole way. I mean right to the hospital. There's something I should confess right away, Dad won't mind I'm sure, we're going to have to call our boy Dennis after the make of lorry that brought me down here."

Dennis grinned. He suspected that was a peace offering as it seemed unlikely the driver would make such a request. Dizzy must have seen the make and thought it would be appropriate under the circumstances.

"I don't understand how you knew to come," Melanie said.

"Your dad phoned me."

"I know what you said, love," Dennis explained. "But I knew you wanted him here and knew he would be if he could. Mind you, that was before I knew about all the fuss with ferries and trains. You did well to get here. Good thing you did because …"

"You had it covered and were doing great." Dizzy stopped his father-in-law admitting he'd nearly fainted. "We'd make a great tag team."

So, no one other than Dizzy had noticed Dennis wasn't really any help at all. He somehow knew his secret was safe.

"Come on …son, let's give Melanie a bit of peace and get ourselves some fresh air."

The lorry driver was still outside the hospital. "I'm almost over my driving hours," he admitted. "I was trying to find somewhere I could park up."

"The bowls club has a big car park and it's just round the corner. I'll sort that out," Dennis volunteered. He might be a bit squeamish, but he could organise overnight parking without trouble.

"Big enough for that?" The driver pointed to a huge Mercedes lorry.

"No problem," Dennis assured him. "Even though I was expecting a different make." He looked at Dizzy and raised an eyebrow.

Dizzy shrugged. "You know me, always getting things wrong."

"Not when it matters you don't," Dennis said, knowing it was true.

2. Surface Charm

"Just coming," Esther called in response to the doorbell. She put down her book and hauled herself out of the chair. "Just a moment," she shouted as she walked down the hallway.

As she reached the door, she noticed the security chain wasn't on. Her son Davy was always reminding her about that.

"Don't open the door without the chain, promise me, Mum?"

She'd promised, so now dutifully clipped the chain into place before pulling the door open a little. She needn't have been so cautious after all, it was that nice boy who'd helped her with her dustbin last week and again yesterday. He'd told her he was working in Sylvester Crescent and passed her house on his journey to work.

"Good afternoon, how are you today?" he asked.

Esther assured him she was well.

"I've been thinking about your driveway and a couple of my mates have got an idea."

Esther looked out at the old concrete driveway. Her husband and son had made a good job of laying it, but that had been a long time ago. Davy had still been at school. Now Esther was a widow and Davy was running the family business. The firm was still called Reynolds and son, although Reynolds and mother would be more accurate.

When the young man had come by the first time, Esther

had been struggling to bring in her wheelie bin. A wheel caught in a crack and it almost overbalanced. Esther could easily have gone with it, had he not come to her aid. The following week he was already wheeling the bin towards the house as she went out to fetch it. He moved more quickly than she did and when the wheel again caught on the damaged surface, it did fall. Luckily, the young man was unhurt. He seemed far more concerned that it could have been Esther.

"You could fall over taking that bin out or trip over one of those loose pieces. Promise me you'll be careful?"

Esther smiled, his concern reminded her of Davy.

"Oh, don't you worry about me, I'm pretty fit."

"I'm glad to hear that, but still be careful."

She had thought about his words and decided she really must do something about the driveway. Davy had offered to do it, but he had problems with his business; she didn't think he could spare the time or the money. Wouldn't he be surprised if she sorted it out herself? The only problem was the cost. She knew it would be expensive.

"What do you have in mind?"

"We could do the job for you. We'd do all the work, you would just have to pay for the tarmac. It would be about £1,500."

"You would do the work for nothing?"

"Well, a few cups of tea would be nice."

"I'll have to think about it."

"Of course, no problem."

Esther did think about it. £1,500 was quite a lot of money, but she would be saving the labour costs. She knew they were usually the highest cost of any job. The young man came back the next day.

"I've spoken to my mates and we're all set. We'll dig up the old concrete on Wednesday and lay the tarmac on Thursday."

"I thought I said I wanted to think about it?"

"Well, yes, you did, but you seemed keen and the thing is there's been an amazing bit of luck. We have to order some really top grade stuff for another job and if we include yours in the deal we'll get a better rate."

"Top grade?"

"Yes, it has special mineral chips so that it's more hardwearing and resists frost. It has a special structure so that it gives extra grip and is less slippery. It will be much safer for you."

Again, she was reminded of her son, this confident explanation that meant nothing to her was very similar to the sales pitches she'd heard Davy use. Esther had never heard of special mineral chips. She thought that all tarmac came with small stones in it as standard. Still this young man actually worked with the stuff all the time, he would know more about it than her.

"It's a really good deal," he said.

"Oh?"

"Yes, just two grand."

"But that's more …"

"More than the regular tarmac, yes, but it's much better quality. It will last longer and there'd be enough to do the side path too."

"Oh, yes I see. I don't even know your name."

"Oh just call me Taff, everyone does."

"So I will see you tomorrow then?"

"Yes, oh and just one thing, could you pay us in cash? It's just that it's easier to divide up than a cheque."

Esther was pleased to see five young men arrive to do the work. She was worried that there would just be two or three and that the work would be skimped. She went out with a tray of tea and her camera.

"What's that for?"

"I thought it would be interesting to take before and after photographs."

The men all appeared remarkably camera shy, so Esther just took a few close ups of the drive surface before taking their empty mugs back in. She took more pictures from her bedroom window, but didn't embarrass the shy young men by making this obvious.

Esther took the men another cup of tea whenever she had reason to put down her books and get out of her chair. She chatted to them for a few minutes as they drank it. They drank a lot of tea, but Esther didn't begrudge it as they were working for absolutely nothing.

The following day the tarmac was laid. She knew it would be a good job as there had been a sound level base under the worn concrete. The men worked hard and were soon finished.

"You have done a good job, now I suppose you would like me to settle up?"

"Yes please, £600 each should do it."

"But that comes to three thousand. That's more than you said."

"Well, not exactly. Perhaps I wasn't clear. £2000 for the tarmac, plus the VAT and of course the delivery charge and the cost of taking the old concrete away. It costs a bit to tip it you know."

"Of course. Now let me see, I'm just paying for the tarmac and other costs? You're not charging for your work?"

"That's right. We wouldn't cheat you, Missus."

"But you would try to cheat your boss? I do Davy Reynolds' accounts. The cost of using the tips is paid in advance. The company who supply the tarmac telephoned me to obtain authorisation for the increase in the order. All costs have been met. All except your labour. As you said you would work for nothing I shall ask my son to dock two days wages from each of you."

Esther smiled, she'd not only solved the problem of her driveway, she'd also solved the problem her son had with his business. He'd known he was being cheated, but couldn't prove it. Thanks to Esther's photos, he now had all the proof he needed.

3. Keep It In The Family

My brother fidgeting with his silk cravat looks understandably nervous. I am marrying him today so I'm a little anxious too.

We're wearing new outfits, in honour of this mutually important occasion. Our suits are crafted from the same material, but I have a long tulip skirt in place of tailored trousers. My smile belies my nerves.

An unusual situation perhaps but we've always been very close; we did everything together throughout our childhood. Why should we stop now we are adults? Our family are delighted for us. Glad my brother eventually found the perfect woman; happy for me finding work I love. Delighted the first service I'm to conduct as registrar is for my brother and the lady who'll very shortly be my sister-in-law.

4. Granddad's Snowman

I place my grandfather's blue hat onto the snowman's head, as carefully as if I was placing it onto that beloved scabby skull instead of this grey ball of compacted snow. I wrap Granddad's tatty scarf gently around the union between the icy head and shapeless body. Standing back I view the result, there is a smile on my face and tears in my eyes.

"We've done it, Granddad, we've built your snowman."

I remember the Christmas before last. My grandfather was staying with us. He bought me a kite. It was a beautiful thing, fashioned in shades of pink and purple and blue, all the colours I love. I was fourteen, with the thoughtlessness of youth I did not thank him for his gift. I didn't care that he'd spent money he could ill afford. I didn't worry about him struggling out into cold streets an arthritic hand gripping the stick he now needed. His disappointment in my ingratitude did not matter, my image did. Kites aren't cool, they're toys for kids.

"What am I supposed to do with that?" I'd sneered, pushing it away "I'm too old for kites." I didn't sulk for long as the next present was a makeup kit from my aunt. That was more like it.

The day after Boxing Day I saw Granddad sat on the sofa holding my kite. He looked very sad and very old. I felt bad then about my ungracious behaviour.

"Granddad, about the kite."

"It's all right, Stephanie love," he interrupted, "It was a

daft thing to get you. I should have just got a gift voucher like your Aunt Mary told me. Would have been easier too."

"So why didn't you?" I realised as I said it, this was hardly tactful "Sorry, I know it's the thought that counts and all that, but it must have taken a while to find this. There's no shops round your way that sell this kind of thing. Why not just get a voucher?"

"I had a kite when I was your age. I loved it. I forget that you think you're all grown up already."

"I'm not really very grown up am I? If I was I wouldn't have been rude about your present. Sorry I upset you, Granddad."

"I was not really upset by what you said. You can throw the kite away but please don't throw away your childhood," then he chuckled and said "I wish I'd hung on to mine."

I asked Mum what I could buy for Granddad to show I was sorry.

She said, "He doesn't want anything that you can buy, just spend a bit of time with him."

I chatted to Granddad more than ever before, and found him interesting. Some of the things he did as a child were hilarious.

He told me about riding his old bone shaker bike down Burnt Hill. It's very steep; Granddad had no brakes except his feet. He was in the next village and barefoot before he stopped. Another time he and his pals had been given the money to get a hair cut. They decided to cut each others and buy sweets instead. They looked dreadful and their parents wouldn't pay for another cut. When he told me about the sweets I could tell by his face that he was tasting them again. I didn't fancy the liquorice pennies or cough candy but the butterscotch and pineapple chunks sounded nice. I found the tin of Quality Street and we made do with a few of them.

Granddad went home in the New Year but he didn't stay there long. He was lonely and finding it increasingly difficult to look after himself. My Aunt Mary finally persuaded him to live with her. He found it difficult to settle in his daughter's house; she fussed.

I saw old fashioned sweets on sale and bought a few for Granddad. I got humbugs and his favourite pineapple chunks.

When I took them round Aunt Mary said, "Sit with him for a while Stephanie whilst I go shopping."

"Sit with me indeed. Treats me like a child that woman."

"Got what you wanted then." I offered him the sweets.

"It was kind bringing me these, take me back, they do."

"Didn't mean the sweets. I meant being treated like a child again. Lots of people have a second childhood. why not you?"

"It's no fun being a kid on your own. What would I do with no pals to play with?"

"Would I do?"

He said I would.

We sucked on our pineapple cubes until the tang was gone and we were left with slivers of sweetness. We flew the kite together, occasionally going down to the beach, but the pebbles were difficult for Granddad to walk on. Once we tried hopscotch, but neither of us was much good at that. During summer we made camps in Stanley Park and took picnics to eat in our secret hideaways. When it turned colder we hired old videos and watched the films he loved, whilst we ate popcorn and nut brittle.

As winter approached Granddad went outside less, was

too tired to play games. We pretended not to notice. Early in December Granddad talked about tobogganing and snowball fights. I knew these would never happen, at least not for him. Granddad believed it though and planned the snowman we would build together. He explained to me exactly how it should be done and persuaded Aunt Mary to find his favourite old hat and scarf for the snowman to wear. Granddad never saw the snow fall, he died the day before Christmas Eve. I arrived too late. They gave me his hat and scarf.

"Your granddad said to give you these, that you'd know what to do with them. Do you?"

"Yes, I know."

There was no snow that winter. It rained on the day of the funeral, cooling and diluting our tears. On the anniversary of Granddad's death it began to snow, just a few flakes but they stayed. A few more fell each day and by Boxing Day there was a fluffy white topping to the whole town. I'm sixteen now, almost an adult. Crunching a sweet I watch as more snow falls onto Granddad's hat on our snowman. I promise myself, and him, that I shall never quite give up my childhood.

5. Downhill All The Way

"Happy birthday, Gran," I said, and handed over the card I'd made her.

"Happy birthday, Mum," my own mother said as she kissed Gran's cheek. She too gave Gran a card, although hers was bought.

"Happy birthday, Mum," echoed Uncle Derek, Mum's twin.

Uncle Derek gave Gran two cards. I guessed one was a card and one was a gift voucher. Probably for somewhere safe and sensible such as a bookshop; that's what he always gives me.

Mum handed over a brightly wrapped package along with her card. I knew what was in there; slippers. I'd tried to reason with her and Uncle Derek, pointing out that Gran deserved a much more interesting present than the same boring things they always got her.

"She gives us such exciting gifts," I pointed out.

"You gran doesn't really need or want anything though, Tilly," Uncle Derek had pointed out.

"As long as we spend the day with her, she doesn't worry about what we bring," Mum added.

I knew Mum was right, but still I was determined not to go for the safe option this year. For the first time ever, I could afford something more extravagant than a nice bunch of carnations.

Mum knew what I'd got Gran; at least, she would have done if she'd believed me when I told her. Gran won't guess what it is, but I'm pretty sure she's guessed what Mum's brought. That doesn't stop her thanking us and won't stop her from unwrapping it in just the same way I've seen her unwrap every gift my family have given her over the years; carefully but with a show of enthusiasm. She removes the paper neatly and smoothes it out so it can be used again. She laughed the first time I told her that was 'green' and explained it was because she was used to making use of everything and wasting as little as possible.

"What's that, if it's not green?" I'd asked.

"I suppose you're right," she'd agreed. "The only difference is that when I was your age we recycled because there wasn't so much stuff available and what there was we usually couldn't afford. It was the poorer people who made do and mended, now it's the rich and trendy who refuse to throw out anything that could be used again."

She's right, I've got much more money than she had as a teenager and my recycling is aimed at saving the planet instead of money, but what does that matter? As long as we re-use and recycle it doesn't matter why. That's not all that's changed since Gran was my age. There's so much more opportunity now. I can do almost anything I want to do. Sure, I might have to train or save up, but almost anything is possible. I've done things Gran wouldn't even have dreamed of doing; often they were only possible thanks to her generosity.

It wasn't until very recently that I realised the reason she'd never trekked in the The Andes, gone swimming with dolphins or taken the Table Mountain cable car was not because she wasn't interested, but because she never got the chance. Instead she got married and had children. It seemed to be taken for granted that was the way things had to be. Maybe they did then, but the world's moved on since Gran was my age.

I'd heard Uncle Derek discussing their upcoming birthday with Mum.

He'd said, "It's all downhill from here, Sis."

They're only forty-five! Why was he so ready to give up? I asked them, but didn't get a sensible answer. I knew Gran didn't feel that way, at least, I hoped not.

First she opened the cards. She laughed at the cheeky one I'd given her. "Oh, Tilly what are we going to do with you?"

She smiled over the pretty flowers on the one Mum had chosen. "That's beautiful, darling."

When Gran opened Uncle Derek's she gasped. "But I know this place!" She held up the card to reveal a picture of a beachfront hotel.

"I thought you might." Derek looked very pleased with himself.

"Your father and I went there on honeymoon. It must have changed a lot, but this picture is just how I remember it."

Gran opened the second envelop from him. It was a gift voucher. She did a far better job of looking pleased and surprised than I'd have managed.

Uncle Derek shrugged. "They're always useful."

We all agreed they were.

Gran opened the parcel from Mum, smoothed the paper and folded it neatly. She removed the lid from the cardboard box and took out a pair of slippers.

"Thank you, love," Gran said. "Just what I needed."

It was true, the ones she was wearing were, well, worn.

"I'm afraid my gift isn't so practical," I said handing Gran another envelope.

She opened it and read the leaflet very carefully. She turned it over and read the back.

"No, Tilly. You didn't!" Mum shrieked as she spotted the picture on the front.

"She didn't what?" Uncle Derek demanded.

"When she said she was buying Mum sky diving lessons, I thought she was joking."

They all stared at me.

"Not lessons exactly, just one tandem jump," I clarified in the hope that made things better. It didn't seem to.

"And you think that's a suitable gift for your grandmother, do you young lady?"

"Yes, I do, Uncle Derek. Gran, it's really not as scary as it sounds. You'd be strapped to an experienced professional and wouldn't have to do anything but watch the view."

"Well, I must say it sounds exciting," Gran said. She didn't sound any more enthusiastic than she had done over the vouchers and slippers.

"It will be. It's something I'd love to do," I told her. "Uncle Derek said something about being over the hill." I caught sight of his expression. "Oh, not you, Gran. He wouldn't say that about you. No one would. And then I thought about the amazing things I've done thanks to you and I thought you'd like to do something different."

"Yes, I remember you saying so," Uncle Derek said. "Mum, that hotel… I expect you're right about the changes. If you like, we could find out. I thought perhaps you'd like to come with me for a short break." He handed her a brochure.

"Oh Derek, how wonderful. Yes, I'd like that very much."

Good old Uncle Derek. Looks like I misjudged him.

"I remember that conversation too," Mum said.

"Slippers are just what you needed," she told Gran. "But I've got you something I hope you'll like as well."

She opened her canvas bag and removed another parcel just like the first one. My theory about there being a cake in there was obviously wrong then. Rats.

Gran opened the second parcel, ripping the paper away and screwing it into a ball. Inside were shiny pumps.

"They're dancing shoes," Gran said.

"Yes. They're starting dance classes in the social club on Tuesday evenings. Shall we enrol?" Mum said.

"Yes please, love. I'd like that very much."

"And how about the sky diving?" Uncle Derek asked.

"I'm not quite so sure about that, but it seems there are a range of experiences I can chose from. Maybe I'll go hang gliding, enjoy a pamper day or try white water rafting. I'll take my time deciding, but I'm sure I'll enjoy whatever I do choose."

"Thank goodness for that. Tilly, will you put the kettle on whilst I fetch the cake your mother made, from the car?" Uncle Derek said.

Hooray, cake!

Gran waited until she'd blown out the candles before asking Uncle Derek, "So who is it downhill all the way for?"

"Me," he admitted.

"And Mum," I prompted.

"You're quite right," Gran agreed. "I know it's nice to get a surprise on the day, but just for once, I think I'd better tell you about your birthday present in advance. I've booked you both a skiing holiday."

I don't know how she knew that's what they'd like, but it was clear from their expressions she'd got it right.

A month later, I took Gran to wave Mum and Uncle Derek off at the airport as they left to go downhill skiing. Then I drove Gran to where the hot air balloon she'd booked was waiting.

"Gran, I'm so proud of you for picking this from the list of options."

"I thought you'd like it better than a pamper day."

"I would, but it's your present."

"One ticket is indeed your present to me, but the second is my gift to you. Now come and get in before I lose my nerve."

6. Dressed To Impress

"Ready love?" Wayne asked as he picked up the car keys.

"Are you going to change?" Pippa asked.

He looked down at his work suit but couldn't see any dog hairs or biscuit crumbs. "Something wrong with this?"

"No. I was thinking of something Mum said." She followed him out to the car.

Wayne drove to the parents' evening at their children's school and she explained on the way.

"Mum was saying that people wear the same outfits for dropping kids at school, work and in the supermarket as they do if they're going out."

"She's right I suppose, but does it matter?" Wayne asked. He hoped it didn't, using his work clothes for social occasions and having them dry cleaned at his company's expense saved him a fair bit of money. Just as well with two teenagers to provide for. There was always something Josh or Lucy needed.

"Not really… But it seems a shame not to have special clothes for special occasions."

"People do. Weddings, big formal ones at least and some people dress up for Ascot or film premieres." He'd almost added cruises to the list but stopped himself just in time.

"Yes for really special occasions. But people could make more ordinary occasions special by dressing up a bit."

He wasn't quite sure if he'd done anything wrong, but took

the safe option and apologised anyway. "I'm sorry I hadn't realised it bothered you when I wear my work clothes out."

Pippa squeezed his leg. "It doesn't, love. I mean, it probably would if we were going out for our wedding anniversary or something, but not for normal things. I'm thinking about Mum's birthday. I want her seventieth to be special."

"She said not to go to too much expense or trouble and I'm sure she meant it." Wayne was very sure. His mother-in-law always meant what she said. He liked her a lot and that was partly because she was so straightforward.

"You're right and she won't complain whatever anyone wears, but I know she'd love it if people were to get dressed up a bit."

Wayne nodded. His wife wasn't always quite as straightforward as her mother, but it was clear she too thought it would be a good idea. "We can. My dinner jacket still looks good as long as I don't try to do it up and you've got that lovely blue dress and Lucy's bridesmaid dress might still fit …" He glanced at Pippa. Mentioning the blue dress might not have been a bright idea. "Or isn't that good enough?"

"It is for us and I can ask my brother and a few others to dress up, but not everyone. I can hardly write 'put a bit of effort into your outfit' on the invites without seeming rude."

"True. And it's not fair to expect people to buy new clothes just for the party either. I'll have a think about it." He couldn't do so immediately though as he had to pay attention to what the teachers thought about their children.

After the parents' evening Wayne suggested they go for a meal at Luigi's to reward the kids for their good reports and Mum for baby sitting. It would be expensive, but he'd learned the hard way that saving every penny wasn't the way to marital bliss. "How about next Tuesday? That will give us time to sort out our glad rags."

"What a lovely idea, Wayne. Thank you," Mum said.

Pippa beamed at him and even the kids reacted favourably when they discovered pizza would be on the menu. It was only later that they asked him what he meant by 'glad rags'.

"Getting dressed up," he explained.

"Like a fancy dress party?" Josh asked.

"No, smart clothes. Not your school uniform or jeans …" It was then he realised they didn't have much else. The same was probably true of other family members. Clearly the task of getting people to dress smartly for Mum's birthday wasn't going to be an easy one. It probably didn't help that the party was to be held in the rather scruffy Community Centre. Sadly anything even slightly smarter was well beyond their budget unless they asked guests to pay for their own food and drinks and he didn't want to do that.

The meal at Luigi's was a success and Wayne had to admit his mother-in-law had been right and dressing up a bit had helped to make more of the occasion. He really must find a way to persuade a hundred assorted family members, neighbours and friends to dress in the manner Mum would feel was appropriate to her very special birthday party.

Wayne did come up with a plan. It sort of involved cruises. Was fate trying to tell him something? A few years ago he'd been made redundant and very fortunately found another job before his compensation payment had all been used up. Pippa had, jokingly he'd assumed, suggested they go on a cruise together, leaving the kids in the care of her mum. Wayne, who wasn't a good sailor, had quickly dismissed the idea as a waste of money and said they'd pay a chunk off the mortgage instead. As he'd put away his suit that evening he'd seen a long, slinky blue dress hanging in the wardrobe.

"I got it for a snip in a closing down sale," she'd assured him. "Can't think when I'll ever get the chance to wear it though."

He hadn't taken the hint and instead sorted out the mortgage payment the following day. It wasn't until he'd experienced a few quiet days at home and found several magazines accidentally left open at adverts he realised he'd made an error. They were for seasickness pills, strong ones, or cruises, short relatively inexpensive ones. When Pippa banged down his plate of ocean pie sending peas skidding across the table and muttered something about the ship having rolled his suspicions were confirmed. He'd definitely upset her somehow.

"Something wrong, love?" he asked.

"No. Everything's fine."

Oh dear, it was worse than he'd thought. Wayne rang his mother-in-law who called him a silly boy.

"How was I supposed to know she really wanted to go on a cruise? When we got that redundancy money and I suggested spending some of it on a bit of a treat for ourselves she wouldn't hear of it except for a few things for the kids. She even worked overtime at the hotel to be sure it didn't run out before I found another job."

"That's true. And you've both been working hard ever since, always putting your children first. Maybe she thought a few days together, just the two of you, was justified?"

"That would be nice," he admitted. "A cruise though?"

"Hmmm, who'd have thought that would interest her? Tell

me, how many times has she watched Titanic now?"

"A million and three. Oh."

"And when's the last time she missed a documentary about either the sea or ships?"

What an idiot he'd been, he realised as he thought of the romances Pippa frequently read. Nine times out of ten they had a ship, sea or someone in nautical clothing on the cover. It also made sense that a person who worked in a hotel might want something slightly different in the way of holiday accommodation.

"OK I should have realised, especially as for once she did actually say what she wanted. It's too late now though, the money's already been taken off the mortgage."

"I'll have a word with her, see if I can explain."

Wayne didn't know what Mum had said to Pippa but it worked. That was just one of many reasons he had for wanting the forthcoming birthday party to be just as his mother-in-law wanted.

He set to work organising food, sending out invitations and trying to think of a way to improve the look of the venue. Pippa's brother was a big help in tracking down people his mother would like to attend and assisting in trying the wine they would serve. He also offered to borrow a few things to decorate the Community Centre. Mum had already provided some money and her son and son-in-law agreed to go halves should more be needed.

On the evening of the party Pippa came downstairs in the long blue dress she'd never before worn. Lustrous curls framed her face and tumbled over bare shoulders. Her skin glowed and eyes sparkled and that dress… wow. What a waste it seemed for her to always pull back that glorious hair into a ponytail and hide herself away under baggy tunics or her stiff work clothes.

"It was worth organising this party just to see you in that," he whispered in her ear as he pulled her close. "You look amazing. As beautiful on the outside as you are inside."

"Thank you, love and thank you for sorting it all out." She kissed him then pulled away to inspect his outfit. "You look great too."

Lucy appeared next, in peach taffeta. The bridesmaid dress looked rather different now she'd grown a few inches and developed a less childlike figure and with a touch of makeup and her hair piled high she looked very glamorous.

"Not exactly fashionable, but it doesn't look quite as bad as I remembered," she admitted.

Josh didn't look quite so happy in his borrowed suit, but he was certainly far smarter looking than was usual.

They set off for the party in the very large and extremely smart car Pippa had borrowed from her boss. They collected Mum on the way. She looked tremendous and he told her so. He guessed she'd spent the whole day having her hair and nails done and enjoyed every second of it.

Mum paused outside the party venue. "I want to thank you for arranging for me to arrive in such style and for all dressing so nicely for my party," she said.

"I don't suppose we'll be the only ones," Wayne said. "After all, this is a very special day."

Pippa looked concerned. Maybe he should have explained his plan but he'd wanted it to be a nice surprise for her too.

Wayne ushered them all inside where they met Pippa's brother and his family. They too were dressed very smartly, much to Mum's delight.

Together the family formed a receiving line to greet their

guests, every one of whom was dressed for such formality. The ladies wore old evening dresses or brand new cocktail dresses, or in one case what was surely a wedding dress. The children were equally well presented. Wayne guessed bridesmaid dresses and prom dresses accounted for many of the girls' outfits.

The men mostly wore dinner jackets with a few in smart military attire where that was appropriate. Uncle George came in highland dress complete with slippers in the same tartan as his kilt, but you can't have everything.

Mum was pleased, delighted even.

"How did you do it, darling?" she asked Pippa.

"I didn't do anything, Mum honestly."

"Everyone has dressed up just for me? How lovely."

Wayne wasn't at all offended or surprised he hadn't been considered as likely to have had a hand in things. The smile on his mother-in-law's and wife's faces was all the thanks he could want.

Pippa led him to a quiet corner. "Come on then, how did you do it?"

He tried for an innocent expression but it didn't fool her.

"Easy. I just put on the invites it was a fancy dress party with the theme of 'dinner at the Captain's table' and promised free drinks for anyone who dressed appropriately."

"Ah, that explains the flags and posters of exotic locations everywhere. They really brighten the place up."

"Glad you approve. Please don't let on it was always going to be free drinks all round anyway."

"I won't." She kissed him and walked away to talk to their guests.

As he watched her retreating back in that gorgeous dress

he knew he'd done the right thing, and not just in regards to the party. On the way back from decorating the room that morning he'd stopped in at the travel agents and booked a three night cruise to the Channel Islands for the two of them. He hadn't yet asked Mum if she'd look after the kids, but he was confident of her answer.

7. A Fresh Recipe

After months working away it was great to be home. I'd missed my wife, Julie, of course and our family and friends, just as I'd known I would. There were other things I'd missed that had surprised me; seeing a face I recognised from my childhood, sharing simple meals at home with Julie instead of eating in a restaurant, a decent coffee and slice of cake.

Because of those thoughts, I initially doubted the evidence of my eyes. But although it was hard to tell who was under the thick coat, woolly hat, scarf and furry boots, it must be Aunt Joanna scurrying into the full force of the icy February rain. What gave her away was the enormous umbrella decorated with a pattern of cakes and biscuits. My aunt loves to bake almost as much as we all love eating the good things she produces.

I stopped my car opened the window. "Aunt Joanna?"

"Hello, Chris. Filthy weather."

"It is, would you like a lift?"

"You don't know where I'm going, you daft chap."

"Doesn't matter. Get in and I'll take you wherever it is."

It didn't take her long to give her umbrella a good shake and get in.

"To the High Street?" I guessed as she fiddled with the seat-belt.

"Yes, thanks."

"Is that new craft shop opening today then?"

"I didn't know you were interested in crafts?"

"I'm not," I explained before she could get some weird gift idea into her head. Cake was what she's always given me every birthday and Christmas and that's exactly what I want every year. "You must have a good reason for going out in such rotten weather and I heard the craft shop are selling a good range of fancy shaped cake tins and pastry cutters."

My wife had suggested it as a good place to buy all future gifts for Aunt Joanna. "Anything that encourages her to cook more cake has to be a good thing," she'd said and grinned.

"That wouldn't get me out in the rain," Aunt Joanna said. "I don't bother with baking much these days."

I gripped the steering wheel: hard. "But why not?" I asked feebly.

"Your Uncle Boris has Coeliac disease. I thought you knew all about that?"

I knew Uncle Boris had been ill, but that was months ago and Julie said he looked fine last time she saw him. "Poor man, has it come back? Is he in a lot of pain?"

"No, thankfully he's not in any pain now, but the disease never goes away. If he ever eats wheat, or anything else with gluten in, he'll get a reaction and it starts all over again."

"Oh, I didn't realise that." Poor chap.

"We did, we were told when he was diagnosed, but I wasn't bothered then. I just cared about him getting better. To start with it wasn't too bad, but now he's feeling fine, it's hard to get him to stick to the diet."

"He doesn't want to cut down on your lovely cakes?" I could understand that!

"He doesn't need to just cut down. He can't eat anything that contains gluten."

"So he can't even have a small slice of cake on his birthday?" What a horrendous thought, especially for a man married to such a fine cook.

"Not unless it's made from special gluten free flour. I sometimes buy it for him, but it's too expensive for the whole family. Because he can't eat any normal cakes, I've stopped making them; it doesn't seem fair."

"No, I suppose not." I didn't want to seem selfish, but it didn't seem fair for Aunt Joanna to be deprived of her hobby; baking cakes for her loving family to eat.

"It's not just cakes. I can't thicken sauces, batter fish …"

As I drove her into town, Aunt Joanna continued with a mouth watering list of food Uncle Boris could no longer eat and which therefore Aunt Joanna would no longer serve at family gatherings. It was scary stuff.

"Which end of town do you need?" I asked eventually.

"I'm going to try in the health food shop and see if they've got bread that's OK for him to eat, so I can make sandwiches for the party on Saturday. You are coming?"

I said I was, although I wasn't looking forward to it quite as much now I knew there wouldn't be any home-made cakes on offer.

"I'll give you a lift home, if you like?" I said.

"I would, but I have a couple of other places to go first."

"So have I," I fibbed. She had enough to worry about without feeling guilty for accepting a lift. "Shall we meet in the coffee shop, then it won't matter if one of us is late."

I decided to do some research into poor Uncle Boris's illness so popped into the library. Everything Aunt Joanna had told me was right, but she'd left something out; the list of food without gluten. Potatoes, rice, maize, corn, fruit, dairy products and soya-based foods were all fine. I'm not much of a cook, but there seemed quite a lot Uncle Boris could still eat.

Reading about the dairy products made me think of the cheese sauce my wife had made for our macaroni cheese a few nights ago. It had been excellent and I told her so.

"Thanks, but your aunt Joanna would probably say I was cheating as I didn't make it the proper way with flour," she'd said.

I gave Julie a call to ask what she had used.

"Cornflour. It's easier than making a roux with butter and flour. Why?"

"Just thinking about something Aunt Joanna said and I thought perhaps you'd done it without flour at all."

"Cornflour isn't ordinary flour, it's made from maize instead of wheat."

I checked the book and found maize was on the OK list. If Aunt Joanna could just change to the cheating way of thickening sauces Uncle Boris could eat them. Not on pasta, but cauliflower cheese was an option. Maybe Aunt Joanna would find more things she could cook if she looked at things in a different way?

By the time she reached the coffee shop, I was innocently looking at travel brochures. "I'll buy you a cake. Although they're not a patch on yours, they're still pretty good here."

"Oh lovely. If we don't tell your uncle he won't be jealous."

When I got back from the counter with our treats, she was looking at the brochures.

"Where are you thinking of going?" she asked.

"It's really difficult. The government have issued a whole

list of places they advise people not to go. Here," I said, handing her the list I'd hastily copied in the library.

"These are all war zones! You wouldn't want to go there, surely?"

"Some of them sound really interesting, but that's not the only problem. Julie doesn't want to go anywhere we have to have a stopover. She's not keen on flying or airports at the best of times and doesn't want two flights to get there."

"But that still leaves so many wonderful places in Europe! You could drive, get a coach, or what about a cruise?"

I grinned. "Exactly!"

"What?"

I think she'd guessed I was up to something.

"This cake is delicious, what's it called?" I asked, waving my sticky, chocolate covered fruit and nuts.

"A Florentine."

"And the thing that man with the moustache is eating?"

Joanna frowned. "Meringue? Are these all named after holiday destinations, is that it? You think I could go to Madeira instead of making Madeira cake?"

"No," I laughed. "Keep trying… See that kid eating the brown lumpy thing?"

"That's a rice cake. Oh! None are made with flour… Yes, Boris could eat all of them. Oh you are a clever boy, Chris. You've given me an idea for the party!"

When we arrived, the table was spread with all manner of party foods. There was pineapple, pickled onion and cheese on sticks, potato crisps, bowls of nuts. I saw sausages wrapped in bacon instead of pastry. What looked like quiche was actually a frittata. The piece de resistance was the birthday cake; a fabulous pavlova instead of a traditional sponge. I didn't notice any sandwiches with or without special bread, but there were so many other things I wouldn't have been able to eat them anyway.

"So where are you going on holiday, then?" Aunt Joanna asked me.

"A cruise," Julie said.

"How romantic." Joanna sighed.

"Glad you think so, my dear," Uncle Boris said. "I've realised how hard it's been looking after me since I was ill and decided you need a break, so I've booked you on a cruise too. Not the same one as them …"

"But I'm not going on my own!" Aunt Joanna protested.

"Of course not. Young Chris here gave me a brochure and pointed out the bit that says they cater for special diets. I spoke to a nice man who assured me they often cater for coeliacs and promised I'd have a choice at every meal, every day."

"Good, I'll make a note of what you like and try making it at home," Joanna said.

"And invite us to dinner?" I suggested hopefully.

8. Grandma's Desk

"Would you like Grandma's desk back?" Poppy asked her sister.

"Don't you need it? That's what you said when you conned me into letting you take it."

"Ooooh, I didn't con you!" She aimed a mock slap not particularly close to Elise's face. "It helped with my poetry. Mainly because I didn't have any other furniture I could write on, but knowing it was Grandma's helped too."

"But now Si is going to buy you a fancy new desk when you move in with him, so I can have the manky old one back?"

Poppy managed a grin. "Manky? Valuable antique you said, and I've polished it, a couple of times at least."

"And soon it'll be mine again, hidden treasure and all." Elise hissed in her best Gollum voice and rubbed her hands together. "The precious is mine."

"Yeah. That or an old gas bill."

"Poppy? Hidden treasure, Grandma's desk? You're giving all that up?"

"It's just a desk, Elise. An old one that won't look right in Si's apartment."

"And is he buying you a fancy new one?"

"I don't need it. I don't write anymore."

Elise put her hand on Poppy's forehead. "This isn't right."

"It is. I've outgrown my childish dreams."

"I wish you hadn't. It was bad enough Si making you leave your writing group, just because they gave you confidence and he was jealous of your friend Mark, but giving up writing entirely? It's wrong. Getting the desk doesn't entirely make up for losing my sister either."

"Don't be daft. I'll be living closer to you than I am now."

"That's not what I mean and you know it."

Poppy did. She'd always been the most impractical of the two. It must be strange for Elise to see her airy-fairy sister grown sensible. She'd get used to it, just as Poppy would get used to her new life with Si. It wasn't true he'd made her give up writing, he'd just shown her how pointless it was.

She'd miss the desk though. On wet Sundays Grandma provided cake and the sisters guessed what was hidden in the secret drawer. A magic spell was a popular choice when they were tiny. Later it was paperwork proving their royal birth, or entitlement to riches. When Poppy first got interested in creative writing she hoped it could be a lost Shakespeare manuscript. Elise once guessed at secret papers from the Cold War, perhaps prompted by the fact she was dating Stuart, a history teacher, at the time.

Grandma had joined in these games, encouraging the fantasies, just as she encouraged Elise's relationship and Poppy's literary ambitions. Grandma had lived long enough to see Elise and Stuart married and one of Poppy's poems earning first prize in a competition. She died leaving the desk to 'my favourite Granddaughter'.

"I always knew she loved me best," Poppy said.

"And me. She loved us both best."

"You're right. So we share the desk?"

Elise took it first as she had a home of her own. Poppy talked her out of it when she'd moved into her bedsit. She'd written hundreds of poems at it. Often she felt the desk itself was inspiring her work. Perhaps those years of childhood imagination were imprinted on it.

When Si first visited her flat she'd explained about the desk and its secret.

"Why not just look in the drawer?" he'd asked.

She'd not known how to answer. After that she'd not mentioned the desk to him until she'd asked him to help carry it down for Elise to take away.

"Don't worry, it was empty," Si said when he returned.

"I know, I cleared it out myself." She'd intended to throw her writing away too, but instead had shoved everything into a big box on top of the wardrobe. Perhaps she should have asked Elise to take that too. Si wouldn't want it cluttering up his place.

"The supposedly secret drawer, I meant."

"What?"

"I thought I'd better check there wasn't anything valuable in there, but there was just this." He scrunched a piece of paper in his hand.

Poppy took it and read the words 'hopes, dreams, possibilities' in Grandma's curly handwriting. "This is valuable, Si. You had no right to take it."

"It's just a scrap of paper. I don't see why you're upset."

"No and you didn't see why I wanted to write poetry either, or why I didn't look in the drawer." She blinked back tears. "The unopened drawer held possibilities, just as Grandma said and just as my poems did. You've taken all that away from me, Si. I'm taking back what I can. I want you to go. It's over."

"Don't be silly, Poppy. All those stamps and the ink for your competitions hardly ever got you anywhere, but you can mess about with your little rhymes at home if you want."

"What I want is for you to leave. Now."

Poppy returned to her writing group where she was warmly welcomed, especially by Mark.

"I've missed you and your verses. Are you still writing on your Grandma's desk?"

"No, my sister has it."

"I remember, you share it with her."

It seemed Mark remembered a lot about her and the desk and the poems she'd written at it.

Elise was delighted to hear Poppy wanted the desk back because she was writing again.

"Will Mark be there to help carry it up?"

"He will, but we're just friends, Elise. I'm off men."

As Mark struggled up the stairs a neighbour's cat shot between his legs causing him to stumble.

"Your secret drawer came out, Poppy. I managed to get it back, but it's jammed shut now."

"Don't bother telling me it's empty. I know."

"It was, but it isn't now. I put something in there."

"What?'

He grinned. "It's not a secret if I tell you, is it?"

Poppy had back everything Si had taken. Her writing, the desk with its secret and all kinds of wonderful hopes, dreams and possibilities for the future.

9. Fiona's Kitchen

It had taken them three attempts to get the colour right. They'd chosen a shade of paint called, 'Honeysuckle'. She'd loved the name and the warm, welcoming shade on the colour chart. Once on the walls it had been more of a hard, cold yellow. Ian had never been too bothered about the finer details of interior decorating, but when he saw she was disappointed, he cheerfully bought another tin of paint in a different shade and put on a coat. That turned out to be bright orange. Fiona had walked in just as he was finishing. She'd tried to look pleased, but he'd taken one look at her face and laughed.

"Will you wash out the brushes, love? I'm off back down the DIY store."

"I'm sorry," she told him when he came back. "I know you'd rather be doing something else when you've finally got a day off, but I do think the kitchen is important, don't you? It's the heart of the home."

"You're the heart of my home, Fiona my love." He hugged her. "But if the colour of the kitchen walls is important to you, then it's important to me."

Fiona sighed, that all seemed so long ago. As she ran her hand over the wall, she remembered a magazine article she'd read after the kitchen had been decorated. She couldn't recall the name of the magazine, or when she'd last had time to sit down and read one, but she remembered the gist of the piece. Something about how a kitchen wasn't just the heart of the home, but how it was also a reflection of the person who owned the kitchen.

At the time, Fiona had felt quite smug. Her kitchen was clean and bright and cheerful. Racks of spices gave it a permanently warm and inviting scent. That day their warmth hadn't been needed as the heat from the oven as she roasted Ian's favourite dish of roast lamb and rosemary had taken care of that. The aroma of spices and sizzling meat had been swamped by the perfume from the bouquet of lilies on the windowsill.

That helped date the article. It had been some time since Ian had bought her flowers. She'd not cooked for him in a while either. She'd not even seen him for almost a month. Was it only two months since he'd first broken the news? There'd been a frantic emotional month of negotiations over money and arrangements for forwarding mail and packing. Then he'd gone. She sighed again; thinking about their separation wouldn't help her now. There was work to be done.

Fiona lifted the microwave and slid it along the counter in order to clean behind it. It had been one of the first things they'd bought when they'd moved in together. She wouldn't think about that either.

Work, that's what she'd concentrate on. She couldn't help her mind wandering though, so she imagined what the writer of the article would think of Fiona, if she looked through the kitchen window now. At least the window was clean, that had to be good.

Perhaps she'd appear organised; she did try to be. It was hard coping on her own, after getting used to Ian's support, but she was managing. Fiona slid the microwave back into its proper position. Well, what had been its proper position.

Soon it, like Fiona, would need to settle into a new home. She'd miss this place, but knew she'd made the right decision. She couldn't stay there without Ian.

The kitchen looked bare, empty. She didn't like to think how well that equated to herself. Without Ian's stereo balanced precariously on the fridge and his pile of books on the table, some of the soul seemed missing from the kitchen. Without Ian, something was missing from her too, but no, she definitely wasn't going to think about that.

She looked at the fridge. Before he'd left, she'd discussed the fridge with Ian. Not argued, they never argued. They didn't argue when he'd bought the ugly great thing with all its special features. They didn't argue when she calmly insisted it stay.

He'd wanted the toaster, she'd let him take it, even though it matched the kettle he'd left behind. They had been a set and were now separated, there was a certain logic in that. Maybe right now Ian was standing in another half empty kitchen that matched him perfectly. The kettle still worked without its partner. She supposed the toaster did too.

Fiona rinsed out the cloth and looked around her. The kitchen was clean. Her possessions were packed and ready to move on. She was too, she convinced herself.

"What about this, love?" the removal man asked indicating the fridge. "Is that coming?"

"No it's not."

"Sorry, love. Your husband said …"

"Despite what he may have told you, that fridge is staying exactly where it is. He's the one who left, so he'll have to manage without it and its fancy chilled drink dispenser. I've told the new people they can keep the fridge."

"Ah, OK." The removal man looked uncomfortable.

Fiona laughed. "Don't look like that. It was a pain to clean, so we hardly used it. It's just that now he's got a really good new job, I reckon we should buy some new kitchen appliances, to go with our new life in Canada."

10. I Know Where The Bodies Are Buried

"Miss Frencham?"

"Yes, dear."

"It's Alan Jones from The News. We spoke last week."

"Oh yes. Thank you for coming to see me."

"A pleasure. Now you mentioned something about a body …"

"I know I shouldn't have said anything, but I had a couple of glasses of wine at the funeral. I rarely drink wine. They give us a glass of sherry here on special occasions, well any excuse really, but it's that syrupy sweet stuff. I can't manage more than a few sips. I'd rather have a cup of tea …"

"Of course, shall I …?"

"Sit yourself back down. Gretel will be round with the trolley soon. Now, where was I? Oh yes, the wine. It made me indiscreet. That wasn't the start though, now I come to think about it."

"So, the start was …?"

"My cousin Greg's funeral. There was a good turn out as you saw. Dozens of people saying what a lovely man he'd been. It reminded me of when Daddy died. Now he had been a lovely man. Popular right to the end. He always had friends and neighbours popping in to chat, bringing him the local news and reminiscing about the old days. I very much doubt anything of the sort happened with Greg. Actually I know it didn't. Visited myself a few times I did. Quite a trek on the buses, but after all he was family and I didn't want him upset with me."

"No, of course not. So the body. You said you know where it's buried?"

"Oh yes, dear. All of them."

"All?"

"Yes. They're all in different places though. Abroad, some of them. I suppose that's part of the problem."

"There are lots of bodies?"

"Hmmm, but there's no need to get excited."

"I'm quite a junior reporter. A story like this could make a real difference to my career."

"I doubt it. I've said the same to other people, but nothing's ever come of it."

"It got covered up? I know Judge Greg Frencham was an influential man. His Honour had many friends in high places."

"Was it you who wrote that kind obituary?"

"No. Don't worry I've no reason to keep the truth quiet. Now tell me about the bodies."

"Not for a minute, dear. Gretel's coming with our tea."

Tea and Battenburg was soon dispensed and their conversation resumed.

"The food isn't bad here, but a bit boring. That's one thing with funerals. You never know what you're going to get."

"You've been to many?"

"As many as I can. Of course it hasn't always been possible."

"No, I suppose not. But some of these bodies had proper funerals which you attended?"

"Had to show my respects. That's what people say isn't it? They go to show their respect for the dead. What about the living? Who shows respect for them?"

"Not your cousin Greg?"

"Well no, but maybe we shouldn't judge him too harshly? He wasn't well. The same can't be said of some of the people at his funeral. Judges, lawyers, doctors, all sorts. You expect better from people like that, don't you?"

"Should be able to certainly. So let's see if I've got this right… Your cousin, Judge Frencham murdered people and his influential friends helped cover it all up?"

"No, of course not, dear boy. He was a lovely man, just like my father. He got old and forgetful and these days that means lonely. It's happened to so many of my family and friends. I visited as often as I could. Often I was the only person they'd spoken to for weeks, yet at the funeral there would be dozens of people claiming the dearly departed would be greatly missed. They showed up to pay respects but hadn't bothered to call in for a chat in years. As I got older and frailer I saw the same thing was happening to me. I started attending local funerals. People always talk to you at funerals and almost always I was invited back for something to eat. Once there, a few quiet words in the right ears that I know where the money, jewels or body are buried guarantees me interesting visitors in the weeks to come."

11. A Question Of Identity

I can't remember much about last night. I hear voices coming from the kitchen; my adoptive mother's and another, deeper, voice snapping out questions. Flashes of last night's activity burst into my skull. Brightly coloured drinks sipped from the bottle. Kissing and angry words. The blaze of headlights. Strident car horns claiming attention. Speed too. I remember incredible speed. Tyres squealing as rubber was left behind. It was loud, frantic, dangerously exciting. Then nothing. No noise, no movement, no thought. I don't want to remember what the nothing was, best just to forget. And not drink. Not so much, not for a while at least.

I roll out of bed and creep into the bathroom. I don't flush the toilet or run the tap. I don't want to draw attention to myself. Whatever the argument is about I don't want to get involved. I'm in no shape for shouting. I clean my teeth with a dry brush, wipe cleanser over my face, before braving a look in the mirror. Yuck! I didn't bother removing makeup last night and most of it's still there, although not exactly where I put it.

My eyes water and brain shudders in response to the sunlight forcing its way in. I close my eyes, but the day cannot be blinked away. Unwillingly, I look again. Outside there's a shiny white Volvo with 'POLICE' neatly stencilled onto the bodywork. Not good. I don't want to face realities of the morning. I want to go back, retreat into the night.

A policeman returns to his car. My father, head dipped

and shoulders sagging, follows.

It's just her downstairs now so I needn't creep about. Everything's an effort; maybe I haven't woken up yet? I hurt all over, my whole body a walking hangover. I put on the clothes I was wearing last night. I didn't want to, but can't be bothered to change now. Don't suppose it matters much, I don't feel up to going out. I'd better try to make some sort of peace with Sarah. Hope whatever I got up to last night hasn't upset her too much. She gets more trouble than she deserves from me. I can't quite forgive her for it, but I suppose it's not her fault that she's not my real mum.

Sarah's crying. Very quietly, but she's really upset. What should I do? I may upset her more by trying to help. That happens whenever we discuss anything more emotive than the weather. Yesterday I accused her of stealing my childhood by separating me from my birth mother. She thinks I'm trying to take away her dreams of motherhood by refusing to be her daughter.

She should have told me. Dad would have, but she wouldn't let him. Dad, of course he isn't really. It seems no one knows who is;probably not even the man himself. Why didn't they tell me the truth? They say my real mum, Sarah's sister, was an alcoholic who couldn't take care of me so they had brought me up as their own. If it's as simple as that, why lie?

The drama of last night needs to be sorted out before other problems can be tackled. I can't believe I got so drunk. What was I doing; trying to prove my parentage? I wish I knew what actually happened. It would sure make explaining a whole lot easier.

"Sorry, Mum," my whispered apology so soft I don't seem to have spoken at all.

"Tracey?" She's looking straight at me, or perhaps through me is more accurate, as I don't think she's seen me.

"Tracey, why did you do it, love?" This question is clearly rhetorical, as she ignores my enquiry into the facts. I try to apologise but she doesn't listen.

A car pulls up outside and she leaps to open the door just as Dad reaches it.

"Sarah, I'm sorry but it was our Tracey."

What was? What did I do?

"Why? Why did she do it? It was finding out about the adoption I suppose."

"Don't talk about me as though I'm not here!" They don't hear me. Don't see me even when I step between them. It's as though I'm not even here.

"You were right; we should have told her years ago," Sarah continues in a whisper.

"She knows you love her, that we both do."

"She thinks I stole her away from her real mum."

"That's what she said but she doesn't really mean it. She knows it's not true."

He's right of course. I blamed her because I wanted to transfer my own pain. She loves me, so made an easy target. I want to explain but can't do it now. Can I do anything? Panic grips me. If I'm not really here, where am I? In the hell I deserve?

They stand close together, drawing comfort from each other.

"Do you want to come to the hospital now?" he says.

Sarah doesn't look as though she does, but she takes her coat from the hook and goes with him.

I follow them and get into the back of the car. They don't speak on the drive to hospital. The motion of the car makes me dizzy. I see the lights again, hear horns, sirens, silence. I want the silence; to sleep and never wake to pain.

I follow my parents into the hospital. Everywhere things are functional, practical and sterilised; yet nothing seems new or even clean. The night has returned. Through dim lighting, half remembered images flash before my eyes. I follow the people ahead, one moment they're my adoptive parents, the next I see my friends dancing in strobe lighting.

We reach a room containing a single bed. Sarah goes to the girl's side, taking a limp hand in her own. My father stands just inside the doorway as if unwilling to be a part of this.

Fascinated I inch closer, will I know her? It's getting dark again and there are bandages, bruises and wires over every part of her that emerges from the dingy bedspread.

Sarah sits close to the girl and whispers.

I can't hear her words but I feel her breath on my cheek.

Sarah repeats her plea. "Tracey, please say something, or blink, squeeze my hand, anything. Let me know you can hear me."

I try to answer her but can't. I would reach out to touch her but my arm won't respond. I try again. Instead of Sarah, I see a glass of lurid cocktail. I don't want that, I stop trying to move my arm.

Hot tears flow. Not mine.

"There is hope love. It's just going to take time." Dad said that, I think. I don't know when.

I sleep.

My parents come back several times. With each visit the

darkness fades, the morning is nearer. Freesias are arranged in a vase on the locker. Their scent is a pleasant change from latex and antiseptic. Something soft is tucked under the sheet. My floppy old fuzzy bear.

"Mum?" I don't know if I really say the word, if she hears. I'll say it again though, thank my mother for bringing the bear.

Yes my mother. Maybe not for the first weeks of my life but certainly ever since. The other one, long dead was never a part of my life. She conceived, carried, produced and abandoned me in a crazy drink induced fog.

Sarah is the one who rescued me from mere existence and gave me a life. The darkness of the night has gone. I open my eyes, ready to face the morning. I squeeze the hand that still clasps mine. I see smiles on my parent's faces through their tears. Their daughter will be OK now.

12. Medical Emergency

I couldn't feel my legs and began to panic. I tried to sit up to check what was wrong with them. A hand placed on my shoulder gently pushed me back on to the bed.

"It's best if you try not to move," the nurse said. "You have suffered a medical emergency." She returned my chart to the end of the bed and then began to wipe my face with damp cotton wool.

I wondered how long I'd been lying here. I tried to read the time on her little watch thing, but it was hanging upside down and I couldn't work it out.

"Would you like a painkiller?" she asked, "I've got some here."

I shook my head. Thankfully I wasn't in pain.

"Nurse Linda, what are you doing?" a voice boomed out.

"I was just offering the patient a painkiller, sister," the girl stammered.

"Well don't, you are not qualified to prescribe medication. Only doctor or I can do that."

"Sorry, Sister, but I …"

"Anyway, why would she be in pain? We haven't operated yet."

Not operated yet? What was going on? I was covered from head to foot in bandages and they hadn't operated yet. Scarier still was the fact that they did intend to operate and they expected it to hurt.

"Why has she got all those bandages on?" sister asked.

"Sorry, Sister, I was just practising."

"Practising? Why on earth were you practising?" sister asked.

I had to admit that was a pretty good question. I was getting a little concerned about this hospital. Until this morning, I'd been feeling perfectly well and ready to enjoy my holiday. I was a little disappointed that it was raining, but that had been the only problem on my mind. I'd mentioned something to Charles about needing a rest and then suddenly I was having my pulse, blood pressure and temperature checked. The next thing I knew I'd been diagnosed with some strange sounding condition that even the doctor had trouble pronouncing.

"Well, take them off again."

The young nurse looked hurt.

"Come on, take them off so that doctor can examine her. We'll let you put the stitches in and put the bandages on after the operation if you do."

I tried to speak.

The sister obviously realised that I'd heard what was said. "Now don't you worry, everything will be just fine. I'll be overseeing everything."

She did sound competent and I relaxed a little. Once the bandages were removed I started to get pins and needles in my legs. Still at least I could feel them. My vital signs were checked again, and the results plotted on to my chart. I was sure they couldn't have altered much in the last five minutes, but kept quiet; at least they were thorough.

"Dr Kuttemopen will examine you now."

I'd laughed the first time I'd heard his name. It didn't seem so funny now.

The doctor who had diagnosed my condition reappeared. As he took the stethoscope from around his neck, I tried not to think how young he looked. Even my GP at home looks as if he should still be in college. There's no reason for the schoolboy looks of this one to be a surprise.

"Please take a deep breath," he instructed as he listened to my chest.

"And breathe out. Yes good, and in again." He nodded in satisfaction.

"Please sit the patient up. I must check her reflexes."

The nurse and sister manoeuvred me so that I was sitting with my legs dangling over the edge of the bed. The doctor produced a rubber hammer and tapped on my knees. He seemed very startled when my left leg shot out in response. I could only hope this was a good sign, suggesting my condition was less serious than he had first thought. My pulse, blood pressure and temperature were checked again. A torch was produced and the doctor peered into my ears.

"Well, Mrs Robins, it's just as I thought. You definitely have antisuperitis. We must operate immediately. Come on everyone, this is a medical emergency."

The three of them rushed around. I couldn't see what they were doing, as every time I tried to move the young nurse would appear at my side, push me back onto the bed and tell me not to move.

"We are ready now," Dr Kuttemopen announced. "Nurse, administer the pre-med."

The nurse spooned some sticky liquid into my mouth, it was very sweet. I was given three spoonfuls.

"Now we shall mark where I shall make the incision."

My stomach was uncovered and the nurse and sister wiped my skin with more moist cotton wool that smelt faintly of Dettol. The nurse held up a tray and Sister removed the cloth. The tray contained an array of equipment, including the rubber hammer and what looked suspiciously like a set of kitchen knives. Dr Kuttemopen took a marker pen from the tray and drew a large cross on my stomach.

"What is it you intend to do?" I found the courage to ask.

"First I shall remove your tonsils."

"That's not where my tonsils are," I pointed out as calmly as possible.

"Oh, hang on."

The doctor disappeared and the nursing staff began the pulse and temperature routine again. The doctor came back, carrying a large book.

"First I shall remove your appendix, then I shall remove your tonsils."

"Oh no you won't," I insisted.

"It's for your own good," he said.

The nurse held me still as he picked up an enormous syringe.

"Now for the anaesthetic."

Just as the doctor loomed over me, I was aware of someone coming into the room.

"I'm sorry, sir, this is a medical emergency," Sister said.

"Yes, next of kin only," the nurse added.

"I am your patient's husband, you have to let me in," Charles informed them.

The doctor nodded his head.

"What's the situation?" Charles asked.

The doctor introduced his team, then described my symptoms, giving the diagnosis and explained what he planned to do.

"Can't it wait?"

"No, this is a medical emergency."

"Well if you're sure, but you might like to know it's stopped raining. We could all go down the beach now and you could operate on Mummy this evening instead."

"Good idea, Dad," the medical team agreed, whilst taking off their uniforms and grabbing buckets and spades.

13. Don't Look Back

'Don't look back,' was Mum's mantra during my childhood. If anything went wrong, that's what she'd say. She refused to hold a grudge or remember anything bad. She was so strong. She wouldn't argue or beg, she just moved on. Usually quite literally. Usually because of a man. Sometimes they proved unreliable, or unkind or bad in some way and Mum would take me and leave them behind. They never got a second chance, especially if whatever they'd done wrong involved me.

She told me about the man who'd offered her a lovely home and easy life if only she'd give me up. Of course it was him she gave up. She did it for me. I don't remember him, or some of the others she'd left because she wanted the best for me. I asked her about them, especially my father.

"No good looking back, love," she'd say. "People have hurt us, sure, and we've had bad luck but we don't want to think about that, do we?"

"I guess not."

"Look forward, that's the way. I've met someone. Someone kind and gentle. He'll provide a home for us both."

He did too. We lived with Malcolm a long time. Long enough for me to call him Dad and stop wondering when we'd be moving on again. Then the arguments started. He wouldn't let me skip school to go shopping with Mum. Wouldn't let me have a boyfriend and stay out late even though every other girl in my class did.

"Thirteen is too young for boys. School is more important," he said.

Mum didn't stand for it. "We can't have him controlling you, love. Holding you back. You have to show him you'll do what you want."

I tried, but Malcolm said I didn't know what I wanted. "A boy will buy you a portion of chips or take you to the cinema, but an education will set you up for the future. Your mother means well, I suppose, but she's not looking forward."

"You're getting boring, Malcolm. Don't you want us to have fun?" Mum said.

"You're her mother, not another teenager. Start acting like it."

After all she'd done for me! I started to tell him, but Mum reminded me looking back was no good. So we moved on again.

The next man didn't attempt to control me. He didn't care what I did or where I went. That's when I saw Malcolm had cared. That's why he'd tried to impose rules. Mum never restricted me in any way, but … she loved me, I knew she did. I tried to look forward.

We were on our own for a while after that.

"This is better, Mum," I said. "Let's stop looking for a man to support us and moving on again when it doesn't work out."

"No looking back, remember?"

"I'm not, Mum. I'm looking forward. I'll take my exams and get a job as soon as I can. Until then, can't we just stay put? Just you and me?"

She hugged me. "You're right. We don't need a man. We'll

do better on our own."

We did too. Mum worked cleaning houses while I was at school. In the evenings we ironed other people's clothes. We lived in a static caravan. If we'd looked back I might have thought it wasn't much of a life compared with some of the places we'd lived. But we didn't look back.

I had boyfriends. None of them lasted long. One slapped me and Mum told me to move on. She was right. I split with him and we stayed in the caravan until I'd passed my exams. One of my boyfriends had a wife, Mum discovered.

"Why didn't I realise?" I asked her.

"He's the one in the wrong, not you. Don't look back and don't blame yourself."

When I began working I had lots of offers, but I always said no until Jake. He didn't give in. He was a good man, I thought. One who wouldn't move on the moment things became difficult. I looked forward to a secure life with a man who loved me.

Then things started to go wrong. He didn't turn up for dates. We argued over silly misunderstandings.

"What's happened, Mum? He used to love me."

"Don't look back, love. Move on. Be happy."

"No, not without him. I love him."

"You can't rely on a man the way you can your mother. Remember how many have let us down? You said we didn't need a man, that it was just you and me."

"Oh, so you're looking back now, are you?"

"No. Yes. I don't want you to be hurt as I was hurt."

"Not being with Jake hurts, Mum. Please help me learn from your mistakes."

"You're right. I made a mistake."

That's when I found out the truth. She'd caused trouble because she was jealous that I'd found the happiness which had eluded her. She'd always been insecure I realised. Not strong; weak.

Between us we straightened things out with Jake. He asked me to marry him. I said yes. We made plans and finally I told Mum.

"I'll be on my own," Mum said. "It's what I deserve. I'll remember you with love. Try not to hate me."

"I don't hate you, Mum. Let's not look back on what you did wrong, but forward to the future."

"I'll try, but I'm not sure I can. I've hurt so many people, myself included. I should have tried harder with Malcolm. When he became a better parent than me I was so sure you'd both see my faults that I ran instead of facing up to them. I wish I could tell him I'm sorry."

"You can, Mum. He's giving me away at the wedding and he too looks back with regret at your break up."

14. Waiting With A Hook

"Here she comes," the assistant announced.

Anne quickly put away her crochet. Not quite quickly enough.

Carole laughed. "That's how I'll always think of you, Mum; putting away your crochet."

"Whereas when I think of you I have so many different pictures in my head." Many of them of places I've sat waiting for you, she could have added. She studied her daughter in her wedding dress. She'd known Carole would look wonderful and wasn't disappointed. "This will be a favourite though."

"It looks good, doesn't it?"

"Perfect. Absolutely perfect."

As Carole changed, the assistant gave Anne a length of the thin ribbon she'd used to trim the dress. Again she didn't quite have it packed away before her daughter could see.

It was a real sign Carole was now grown up that she didn't roll her eyes as Anne packed away her work. She wasn't more patient, just more tactful. "What are you making anyway? You never would say."

"You'll find out soon enough."

"I hope it is soon."

Anne just smiled. She'd learned to crochet during the last few weeks she was pregnant with Carole. It had been a hot sultry summer and Anne was restless and eager to have the birth over.

Her mother-in-law had advised, "You'd be best off learning to enjoy waiting. I'll teach you to crochet."

Learning to handle the hook and wool had distracted Anne for a while and stopped her fretting. By the time Carole was born she'd produced one neat square, and quite a few weird shaped pieces. She discovered the crochet hook was the ideal thing to carry in her handbag so she could make the most of any free moments. At first there were few of those, but Anne created another square when baby Carole had a fever and Anne sat with her through the night. She made another while Carole spent her first morning at school without her mum and one after Carole fell out of a tree and had an operation to set the bone in her arm. One way and another Anne had spent a lot of time waiting for her daughter.

As Anne's skill with the hook increased she incorporated different materials. One square was made using a strip of Carole's comfort blanket. She used the trim from her first party dress and her school uniform. Various hair ribbons were also incorporated. Anne crocheted as Carole took her exams, went on her first date and took her driving test. She made another the night Carole and Liam got engaged. That one was made from strands of carrier bag from the shop where they'd met and had been really tricky to work. Anne backed the square with cloth as she didn't think the plastic alone would hold much heat.

All the squares she'd made so far were laid out in Carole's old bedroom and neatly stitched together. Just three more were needed to complete the blanket she would give Carole when the time was right. One square would be made from a combination of the ribbon she'd just collected and the blue silk Liam's wedding waistcoat was made from. Another would be made using trimming from their wedding gifts and party favours. The final one wouldn't be Anne's responsibility.

On the day, just over a year later, Anne learned she was to become a grandmother, she gave Carole the beautiful blanket of crocheted squares and a photo album. Each page of the album corresponded to a square on the blanket. Most pages held a photograph of Carole, details of what she was doing at the time and an explanation of the materials used in the crocheted square. The first page showed Anne's scan from when she was carrying Carole. The square was made from the same delicate pink wool as her gran, Anne's mother-in-law, had used to make her christening shawl.

"This is fantastic, Mum! It must have taken years."

"A lifetime!" She explained she'd made a square every time she waited for Carole.

"Now I understand why I've seen you using your hook so often."

"It's not really mine. It was your grandmother's and now it's yours." She indicated where the final square of the blanket was missing. "That's for you to fill in."

"Can you teach me now? I can't wait to see it finished."

"You'll have to wait, at least until I can buy suitable wool." Anne would take her time selecting the perfect yarn for the shawl she'd make the baby. She'd take her time teaching Carole to crochet too, although it would be the baby's job to teach her patience.

15. Hanging Up My Boots

I can't be paralysed. My wife nursing me – what sort of life would that be for her? I don't want the children seeing their big strong father withering to nothing in his wheel chair. My army pension will be enough to live on, but not to compensate for my lack of dignity. If I'd been wounded in battle things might be different. I'd have some pride then. A medal on my chest distracting eyes and minds from the wheels on my chair. This wasn't caused fighting for queen and country but the Army's honour at rugby, and we weren't even winning.

"Alec! Say something mate."

I don't want to respond to say, "It's OK I'm fine," when I know I'm not.

"Speak you old devil. You're not dead mate, I can see you breathing."

"One, two, three, lift!"

They move me onto the stretcher, carry me off the field.

"Alec. Mate, come on you turkey say something, anything."

"Didn't think I hit him that hard."

"Don't know what happened, he just seemed to collapse before me."

Other players are all talking at once. None of it makes any sense to me.

"Wasn't your fault leek-lover, winded him maybe as you

came down on him."

"Taff's fault or not he'll pay for that chunk out of old grizzly's thigh."

"Mate, please mate."

The voices are all around as I'm carried to the dressing room. I want them to go. Leave me. I'll have to say something. They'll think I'm OK then and get on with the game. I'll make some quip to get them out.

"I can't move my legs." Was that pitiful bleat really me? Why had I said it, voiced my fear?

"Of course you can't mate but hang on, they'll sort you out at hospital."

"Is that all you can say, Boyo? You're going soft."

"Come on lads, let's show this idiot we can win the game without the likes of him falling over his own feet and tripping people up."

"Yeah be a damn sight safer without dozy fools like him lying all over the pitch."

Then there was quiet. I opened my eyes then, to see Stumpy. The panic I was feeling must have showed.

"Don't worry, mate. The ambulance is on the way, they'll sort you out. You'll need gas and air stuff, like that."

"Stumps mate it's no good pretending. I know."

"Know what?"

"For Christ's sake do I have to spell it out, I'm paralysed."

"No you're not, mate."

So calm, so certain, so wrong.

"I know. I can't move my legs. There's no pain. I can't feel anything at all."

"If it's pain you want pops don't worry they'll be plenty of that once they try sorting this little lot out."

The ambulance crew and paramedic have arrived now. I feel faint. Just want to sleep. People are talking about me but I can't understand their words. Stumpy talks about 'seeing to' my wife. Always knew he fancied her; I'll see him off though. I'm not going to die and let that letch get hold of her.

"… as quick as we can. Then you can have gas for the pain, we'll dress the wounds on the way to hospital."

They're talking to me.

"I won't need pain killer, it doesn't hurt. I must be completely paralysed."

"No pops, your leg is a bit of a mess but reckon you'll walk on it soon enough, you ready then?"

"Go ahead."

I've no idea what I'm agreeing to except that it will be quick and then they'll get me to hospital. Perhaps Kate will be there. I want to see her.

There are people holding me by the shoulders and at my legs and feet. I can feel a kind of tugging. I try to open my eyes to see what's happening. The effort is too great. I probably wouldn't see past the people holding me down. Why hold down a paralysed man? Aaargh! The pain! Pain so strong I can't tell if I'm freezing or on fire. Make it stop. Let me die. Let it be over. I can't locate it, it's everywhere. Now it's just in my leg. Feels as if my leg is bigger than my body. Pain, that's good. I don't know why pain is good just know that it is.

"Mr Frances, can you hear me?"

"Yes."

"You're in hospital, do you remember what happened?"

"No. Yes. My legs something about my legs, I can't move

them."

"No they are strapped up. Do you know what day it is?"

"Wednesday." What difference does that make?

"Would you like something for the pain?" I wouldn't, pain is good. "Yes." I'm tired.

"Alec, I'm here, it's OK."

Kate's voice but I don't know where she is.

My leg's really throbbing, my shoulder too. Something small and hairy has died in my mouth. My eyes aren't focussing. What the hell have I done this time? After every lad's night out I swear I'll never drink again and always I stick to it. Sometimes for a whole week. I'm in hospital so it must be bad; perhaps I will go a bit steadier in future. No it wasn't the beer, I remember now. Rugby. My legs, I'm paralysed. How could I have forgotten that?

It comes back now, a horrible crack when Taffy landed on me. The air pushed from my lungs then, as I managed to breathe again, I couldn't move my legs. No that's wrong it started with my legs not working that's why I fell. That can't be right you don't just become paralysed. The noise, that must have been my spine. Oh I don't know, too tired to work it out.

It hurts, hurts a lot and I was wrong. Pain is not good. It's not fair. If I'm going to be paralysed I shouldn't have pain too. Taff 'll be eating his leeks as soup for the rest of his life once I get hold of him.

"Mr Frances, I am Dr Nasser. I would like to explain your injuries and future treatment to you."

"It's OK, doc. No need to be tactful with me, I know I'm paralysed. There's nothing you can do about that."

"You have a serious injury but are certainly not paralysed.

What made you think you were?"

"Couldn't move my legs from the second it happened, or feel them, still can't move them of course. Hurt though. Oh don't you dare smirk at me! What rotten sort of bedside manner is that?"

"Sorry, Mr Frances. Perhaps I'd better explain. You're obviously not fully aware of events. You slipped during the match causing the man behind to fall on you, completely winding you, dislocating your knee and breaking the other leg. During this you managed to tread on your own foot and caught a stud from one boot in the lace hole of the other. This meant they were locked together. Sadly your boots will never walk again. Fortunately you will."

16. Why?

Rona watched the small boy kick the fallen leaves into a neat pile. There weren't many. Presumably the railway staff swept them up in case they were the wrong kind and blew onto the track.

The child ran back to his mother, who occupied the only other bench on the small platform.

"Why all the leaves falled down?" he asked her.

"Because it's winter, love. They always fall off the trees at this time of year."

"Why is it winter?"

"We have to have different times of year or it would never get to be your birthday or Christmas and you wouldn't get presents."

The child ran off, scattered the leaves and returned. "Why has that lady got a suitcase?" he asked, pointing at Rona.

"I expect she's going away somewhere, just like us."

"Why is she on her own?"

"I don't know, love. Don't point though, it's rude."

"Why is it?"

Rona could see the mother's patience was wearing thin. Would she have been like that? Possibly now and again. How she'd have loved the chance to find out.

"The leaves are blowing about," the mother told her child.

"Come back," he called, chasing after them.

The mother turned to Rona. "Sorry about that. 'Why?' it's all they ever ask, isn't it?"

Rona nodded as though she'd been lucky enough to have a child. As though she'd been constantly pestered with the question. She couldn't remember ever being asked it. Carl hadn't when she left. It's not a question she'd asked him, or herself, either.

She had asked Carl other questions. "Who is she?" she'd demanded after spotting him with his arm around a pregnant young woman. Not immediately; she'd been too shocked at his betrayal to speak at first. Later she thought, hoped, she'd misunderstood the situation. Then she'd discovered bank withdrawals, smelled perfume on him when he'd said he was playing golf and noticed he'd stopped leaving his phone unattended.

"Her name's Natasha," he'd said. He sounded almost proud.

"The child is yours?"

"Yes."

"And you've been spending our money on her?"

"Yes." Oddly that's when he'd looked the most ashamed. "I know I should have told you about her, asked about the money. She said so too, but I just couldn't."

"So sweet of her to think of my feelings!"

"She's a sweet kid." It seemed he hadn't registered her sarcasm.

"How long have you known her?"

"About six months."

That was the most painful of his answers. Natasha looked, to Rona's jealous eyes, to be around six month's pregnant. How unfair that, after all their years of trying, Rona hadn't conceived but Carl had got this girl pregnant straight away. Presumably without trying, though she didn't know about that. She'd thought she'd known him so well, but clearly not.

When he'd shared her sadness each month as they realised no baby was coming and again when the doctor said it was very unlikely one ever would, she'd thought he'd felt as she did. That it was a disappointment, but one they could live with as they had each other. Now he no longer had to be disappointed and she no longer had him to lean on.

Six months back, things had looked so very different. Her husband was by her side. She trusted him and knew, or believed she knew, that he loved her as much as she loved him. Rona had been as wrong about that as she had been about the fact that she was at last, against all the odds, pregnant. She'd been so, so happy in her ignorance. Then she'd discovered it was all lies. Her body was lying to her, promising a child and delivering an early menopause. Her husband was lying to her, had cheated on her.

Rona yelled bitter, hurtful words which did nothing to reduce her misery.

"It's not like that," Carl tried to say. "What I feel for her …"

"I don't want to hear about her!"

Rona's emotions and hormones were a mess. Her life in tatters. She'd struggled free of his arms and ran upstairs. She shoved clothes into a suitcase and left for the train station slamming the door behind her.

It was only now she realised she had no plan, no direction. Nothing.

"Why are you crying?" the boy asked Rona.

His mother told him not to bother the lady.

"I'm crying because I'm sad," she told him.

"Why are you?"

Good question. It wasn't because she was leaving her home. That was her choice. It wasn't really because of the child which would never be. Of course she was upset, but she'd grieved gently over her infertility for years and intensely for the last few months. It was because she was facing it all alone. That was something she'd never thought she'd have to do. Carl, she'd been sure, was the one thing in life she could rely on.

She didn't really know what had gone wrong. She hadn't asked, hadn't let him explain. Perhaps she should. Maybe it would help her? Even if it didn't, at least she could pack properly. Although a long way from happy, Rona felt a little calmer. A little more as though she had some control over her life. She would go back home, seek an explanation, make financial arrangements and think about where she would go and what she would do.

Rona first approached the boy's mother. "Would you allow me to buy him some sweets?" She gestured to the vending machine.

"That's kind, but …"

"No sweets from strangers?"

"Best not."

Rona extracted a note from her purse. "Take this then and buy him a little something …please."

The mother hesitated, then accepted. "Thank you. Noah, thank the nice lady. She's given you a present."

"Thank you, nice lady."

Rona was glad neither of them asked why she'd made the gesture. Perhaps Noah asked his mum why the lady wasn't waiting for a train anymore but if so, Rona was too far away to hear.

Carl was still sat on the sofa where she'd left him. He'd made himself a coffee, but hadn't drunk it.

"Why, Carl? Why has all this happened?"

"What part of it?"

"All of it. Everything to do with… Natasha."

"I've tried to explain before, so many times, but I didn't want to hurt you. I've made it worse though, haven't I?"

Rona nodded. It seemed to her to be about as bad as it could be and most of it was Carl's fault.

"As I said, I only found out about her recently."

"Met her you mean?"

"That too. She didn't know who her father was until a year or so ago. It came up when she got married and she'd got a copy of her full birth certificate. I wasn't named, but neither was the man she'd believed was her father and she started asking questions."

"That doesn't make any sense. Why would anyone think your name should be on her birth certificate?"

"I'm her father."

"But… You mean Natasha's?"

"Yes. It happened before I met you, of course. I didn't know her mother was pregnant and Natasha herself only recently found out about me." He picked up his coffee mug, but put it down again without taking a sip.

"I've spoken with her mother and it is true, I'm sure of that. I wanted to tell you, but then you thought you were pregnant. I worried it might overshadow your joy. Our joy." His face showed no trace of that happy emotion. It looked instead as it had when they'd realised they had no cause for celebration.

Rona sat beside him and waited for him to continue.

"Then when we discovered the truth I thought it would be harder still for you to learn I had a child. Just as I felt maybe I could tell you, Natasha told me she and her husband were expecting a child. It seemed too cruel to tell you that."

"So you lied to me instead?"

"I'm so sorry."

She saw that he really was and now at last she knew why. It was because he hadn't wanted to hurt her. He'd preferred to hide away his own happiness at having a daughter rather than add to Rona's misery. And why was that? Because he loved her.

She'd been wrong about Natasha, but right about him.

"So you're going to be a grandfather?"

"Yes."

"And you're a father?" She knew the answer now, but wanted to allow him at last to talk about Natasha.

"Yes. Yes, I have a daughter."

"Who is a sweet kid who thought you should tell me the truth?"

"That's right."

"So, do I get to meet her?"

"If you'd like to."

"I think I would, yes."

Carl didn't ask why.

She hoped he knew. When he pulled her close and told her that he loved her, she was sure that he did.

17. Adam's First Case

Adam adjusted the focus of his binoculars. He'd promised community police officer PC Marks that he would carry out observations, because of the recent burglaries in the area. Adam is an unofficial deputy and in training for when he's old enough to join the force. It was already dark outside, and Adam had been on stake-out since tea time. He could see people in the garden, but they weren't burglars. It was his mum and dad. He went to see what they were doing.

Mum was holding a shiny red bicycle and a torch. Dad was doing something to the wheels with a spanner. The bike was a really good one, with lots of gears and it had metallic paint. It must be for his older brother Jimmy. Nine year old Adam knows a big bike like that can't be for him.

"Please don't tell Jimmy, it's a surprise," said Dad.

"Jimmy's getting a new bike for Christmas?" Adam asked.

"We're helping Santa. He can't get to everyone's house in one day so he asked us to help," Mum explained.

"So is Santa real then? You saw him?"

"Santa's real, Adam," said Mum. "He's just not quite like the man in the story books."

"Does he have a red suit and a beard?"

"Only when he's working. It's his uniform."

As soon as Mum said 'uniform', Adam thought of his hero. "Like PC Marks' uniform?" he asked.

"That's right."

"And like a policeman he can't do everything on his own," Mum said.

"So are you helping Santa with his enquiries?"

"Granny did that bit," Dad laughed. "You remember that she asked you to write letters to Santa?"

"Yes, Dad."

"Well Jimmy asked for a bike. We bought it to help Santa."

"So mums and dads are like special policemen?"

"Well, sort of. Will you promise not to tell Jimmy about the bike?"

"Yes, Dad."

Adam knew that if you are told a secret you should never tell, and if you make a promise you must always keep it. Except if it's bad and someone might get hurt, then you should tell a responsible grown up, like a teacher or a policeman. He wouldn't tell anyone about Jimmy's bike. That was a good secret.

"Mum, if Santa doesn't bring all the presents what does he do?"

"He takes care of the magic of Christmas."

"What's that?"

"It's all the good things that happen, but you can't buy in shops."

Adam was happy. When Granny got them to write to Santa, Jimmy had asked for the bike. Adam had asked to be a policeman. He knew he couldn't be a real one for years and years, but he wanted to be a special agent or something. He'd seen programmes on the telly where the police were confused but children helped round up the criminals. Adam wanted to do that. He wanted to go on stake-outs and look for clues and take finger prints. When he wrote the letter, he'd thought it was a waste of time, because it wasn't the kind of present that could be wrapped up and put under the tree. He didn't think Santa was real either. How could one man deliver all those presents? He also thought it was odd that no one saw him except at Christmas; if you went round dressed in bright red you'd expect to get noticed. Now that Mum and Dad had explained, he hoped he would get what he'd wished for.

When Jimmy came home, the first thing he said was, "Mum, do you know where my football boots are?"

"I didn't think you would be needing them. I've tidied everything up."

"Wasn't going to play, but they said they need me. The usual goalie's got a cold."

"When's the game?" asked Mum.

"Next week, but I need the boots to practice. Where are they?"

"In the shed," Mum told him.

Adam remembered the bike was hidden there. He had to stop Jimmy going to the shed. "I'll get them for you." He jumped up and took the key from the hook.

"Thanks, Squirt. I'll get changed. You can come and be linesman if you want."

Adam loved being linesman, ever since Jimmy called the officials 'football police'.

It was dark in the garden, so Adam took a torch. The shadows seemed to move about as he walked. One shadow looked just like a big man trying to look into the shed. As Adam got nearer, the shadow came towards him. It was a man. He grabbed Adam's arm.

"Shh kid, keep quiet, there's a good lad."

Adam was frightened, he tried to think what a policeman would do. "Who are you and what are you doing here?" he asked bravely.

"Don't worry, Kid. I'm Santa."

"Really?"

"Yeah, don't be fooled because I'm not wearing the red suit, I'm keeping that clean for Christmas Eve."

So Mum was right! "Have you come to look at Jimmy's new bike?" Adam asked him.

"Yes, and I need to check any other things your family have bought recently."

Adam unlocked the shed and showed Santa the bike.

"Nice shed this," Santa said, as he walked around looking at Dad's tools and ladder. "It's clean and dry and you keep it safely locked up. It gives me an idea. There are more presents I need to get for people in this street. Perhaps I could store them here?"

"I expect so, I'll I go and ask Mum and Dad."

"No," Santa shouted. "I mean, you can't do that, I've got presents for them too," he explained.

"But if we don't tell them, how will you get in? PC Marks says we must lock everything, because of burglars."

"You can get me a spare key. What are you doing tomorrow?"

Adam said, "I'm going to the library after lunch."

"Meet me there at two then. Remember don't tell anyone, it's our secret. If you break faith with Santa it damages the Christmas magic, and some people won't get what they want."

"I won't tell, Santa. I promise."

While Adam was in the library Santa borrowed the shed key and got a spare made. As Adam walked back to find Mum in the car park, he met PC Marks.

"Hello there, Deputy," the policeman said.

Adam answered, "Hello. Have you arrested anyone today?"

"Not yet, I'm still looking for that burglar. Have you seen anything suspicious?"

"No, officer. What has he stolen?"

"All kinds of things. TVs, money, jewellery, even a trombone. You keep an eye out."

"I will," promised Adam.

That evening Adam checked that Jimmy's bike was OK and looked to see if Santa had brought anything else. He had; TVs and a trombone. Santa must have found out what had been stolen and was getting new ones for people.

The next day PC Marks came around to tell them about more burglaries. When he'd gone, Adam went to the shed and saw the same kinds of things as he knew had been stolen. Some didn't look very new. Odd, he expected Santa to give new presents. But there were so many now; perhaps he didn't have enough money for new things?

The following day Adam found a big bag, like the one Jimmy used for football. In the bag were lots of rings and necklaces and bracelets. They weren't in boxes like the necklace that Dad bought for Mum once. They were all jumbled together. There was another smaller bag inside. That was full of money, all in notes. There was too much to count. If Santa had so much money, why wasn't he buying new presents? Why was Santa bringing exactly the same kind of things that some burglars were taking away?

That night PC Marks was on TV explaining about the robberies.

"The thief has taken some very distinctive items including unusual brooches." He showed pictures of metal birds covered in jewels. "He's also taken malt whisky and the trophies from the golf club."

Adam thought he had seen birds like that in the shed. He wanted to go and look, but it was bed time.

The next day Adam, Jimmy and Mum all went shopping. Adam saw a sign for Santa's grotto. He wanted to go and ask Santa about the things in the shed. There must be a reason.

"Come on, Squirt. Aren't you a bit old for all that?" Jimmy asked.

"All what?"

"That's just some bloke dressed in a suit. It's all a con."

"It's not the real Santa?"

"No."

Adam looked at the poster. Jimmy was right. The man in the picture was nothing like the man who was putting presents into the shed.

"But they say here it's the real Santa. That's lying."

Mum said, "It's more like telling a story."

At home, Adam went straight to the shed and looked in the sports bag. The jewellery birds were the same as the pictures that PC Marks had shown on TV. There were also some bottles and shiny trophies. Adam looked carefully at the trophies; they had lists of names and dates engraved on little metal shields. One of the names was their neighbour's, he had won the golf tournament last year. The things in the shed weren't just like the things that had been stolen. They were the same things. That man wasn't really Santa. He was pretending; lying. He must be the burglar.

Adam knew he must do something. The man was putting stolen things in Dad's shed. Dad might be arrested and Adam would never get a job with the police if he was a criminal's accomplice. The man was lying, he wasn't really Santa. The lies might damage the Christmas magic and if it did Adam's wish to be a policeman would never come true. Adam had to stop the burglar.

Adam ran indoors to tell his parents. He nearly did, but what if he was wrong? Then Santa would be arrested and there'd definitely be no Christmas magic. He couldn't risk letting Mum and Dad look in the shed, Santa said their presents were hidden inside. Perhaps some of the rings were for Mum. She'd like that and he knew Dad really wanted a golf trophy. Adam didn't know who to ask. He had promised not to tell his parents about the things that were hidden. He'd promised not to tell Jimmy anything about the bike. He couldn't tell a teacher because it was a school holiday. He must tell PC Marks. Adam was nervous about this. If he was right it would be great, he would have helped the police catch a criminal. If he was wrong, he would look like a silly idiot for not knowing the difference between burglars taking things and Santa giving them.

Adam remembered that PC Marks had come to school and used a special pen to write postcodes onto all the children's bikes. If he could get him to do that to Jimmy's, he would see the other stuff in the shed and know what to do. Adam knew that Mum had written down PC Marks' mobile telephone number. It was only to be rung for something important. He waited until Mum was upstairs, took a deep breath and rang the number. Luckily PC Marks was on his beat quite close to Adam's house. He said he could come round straight away.

"Well, Deputy, where's this bike then?"

Adam led the policeman down the garden path, to the shed.

PC Marks looked inside the shed, and asked Adam if he had known what was in there.

"Yes, but the man pretended to be Santa and made me promise not to tell. I had to think of a way to make you find the things without breaking my promise."

"You did very well."

The policeman then spoke into his radio and then asked Adam, "Can you help even more by coming to the station and making a statement?"

Adam and his mum were taken to the station in a police car. A policewoman asked Adam lots of questions and wrote down all his answers. Mum didn't say much.

PC Marks explained to Mum and Dad that they would like help to catch the burglar. "Adam, will you help me on my stake-out?"

Of course Adam agreed.

PC Marks came round just after tea time. The officer and his young deputy waited in Adam's bedroom. The door was kept open so that Mum could come in with sandwiches, cakes and biscuits. She made cups of tea for PC Marks and hot chocolate for Adam. The policeman explained that it was important to have plenty of food and drink whilst working, to keep their energy levels up. Adam thought it was a bit like an extra special midnight feast. He was able to ask PC Marks a lot of questions about becoming a policeman. He learnt that it was important to work hard at school, as he would need to be able to read and write statements and get every detail correct.

PC Marks let Adam look at his pocket book. Adam decided he would keep notes too, and carefully wrote out the date and time and all the details of their observation. PC Marks said that Adam was doing that very well, and he would have plenty of experience with police routine by the time he was old enough to join the force. He then explained again everything that would happen if they saw the burglar.

"This is your case, Deputy. You'd better be the one that decides when to make the arrest," PC Marks said.

PC Marks also explained how it was important to be a nice person and to get on with all sorts of different people. "We rely on co-operation from the public, you see, deputy."

It was Adam's job to liaise with the public in this particular case. He thanked Mum for the snacks. He spoke to Jimmy and Dad who came upstairs for regular updates. Adam thought they came about as often as there were adverts on the TV. Adam didn't have much to report, even when they had been watching for ages and ages and it was gone past Adam's bedtime. They didn't go to sleep, but kept observation on the shed from the bedroom window.

Adam watched carefully. He thought he saw something move. PC Marks tapped him on the shoulder and pointed, he had seen it too. They stared through their binoculars and they saw the burglar. He was carrying a large bag. They saw him walk up to the shed and put the key into the lock. PC Marks made a call on his radio. Then he held it for Adam to give the instruction.

"Go, go, go," Adam shouted.

Suddenly there were lights and lots of police. The burglar was quickly arrested. Handcuffs were put on him and he was taken away in a special police van.

On Christmas Eve, PC Marks and a police inspector came to the house.

"We are so pleased with your help that we wish you could join the force straight away," the inspector said. "You can't quite yet, but we'd like to give you a special training day so that we know we can always rely on you."

"Yes please," Adam said, "When do you want me to come?"

"As soon as possible, I'll speak to your mum and dad and see what we can arrange."

Adam had a lovely Christmas. He ate ever such a big dinner, but he still had room for chocolate log, Christmas cake and strawberry trifle for tea. He was given some really nice presents, there was even a parcel from the police station. It contained a new pocket book, a magnifying glass, and lots of chocolate. That must be to keep his energy up. He decided to take some on his training day, to share with PC Marks. Everyone was pleased with the presents he had given them. He thought granny liked hers best, it was a papier-mâché vase that he'd made himself. She smiled a lot when she saw what it was.

On Christmas night, Adam was just as excited as he had been the night before, because he knew that in the morning he would start his police training. On Boxing Day, just after breakfast, Adam and his family were collected by a police car and driven to the police station. They were met by PC Marks and the inspector. They were taken on a tour round the station and were allowed to go everywhere. They stopped for a tea break in the police canteen. It was then time for Adam to start his training.

First, he had his finger prints taken by a sergeant. Once he knew how it was done, he took fingerprints from PC Marks.

Mum was given the sheet of paper with Adam's prints on, so that she could take it home for him.

Adam was taken to see the police dogs. A police dog handler said that Adam could help him exercise one of the dogs. They took Fuzz outside, and his handler showed Adam how to put on the harness that is used when they track criminals. Just as his family were stroking the dog, a man ran up and stole Dad's car keys. The dog handler called to the man to stop, when he wouldn't the policeman called a warning to him and then released Fuzz. The dog ran straight to the man and jumped up and caught hold of his arm. The thief stopped then. The policemen and Adam all ran up to put handcuffs on the man. It was PC Marks! He had been pretending to be a thief. He explained that this was how the dogs practised. He showed Adam that he had some padding on his arm, so he hadn't been hurt.

Once they were back inside the police station they were taken to look at a police cell. They all went in and sat on the hard bed. PC marks let Mum out first, then he and Adam locked his brother and Dad in a cell. They let them out again of course, but not until Mum had finished laughing.

They were taken home again in a police car. Adam was allowed to switch on the lights and siren as they drove up to his house. Now that he had helped catch the burglars and saved the magic of Christmas, Adam was ready for his next case.

18. Good And Proper

"What made you first suspect the waiter might not be all he seemed?" asked the judge. He glared over his half moon glasses, scaring Daz, good and proper

"It was the way he'd knotted his tie, your honour," the plucky defendant tried to explain.

"But the waiters at The Salmon-Ella wear bow-ties."

"Yes, your honour," Daz confirmed.

"One doesn't knot a bow-tie man! One ties a bow-tie, unless one is a total charlatan and wears one of those ghastly elasticated polyester things."

Good, Daz thought. The judge was properly annoyed now and not with him. "Exactly, your honour."

"And don't keep calling me your honour. We're not in court and you're not a defendant whom I am questioning," the honourable Sir Martin Pinkley-Smythe insisted.

"No, sir," Daz said, despite not quite believing the judge meant what he'd just said.

There were a lot of things Daz didn't quite believe. One was that he'd had the nerve to ask Portia Pinkley-Smythe out on a date. Another was that she'd not only agreed to go to dinner with him, but had also kissed him good and proper. He'd had no trouble believing the evidence of his own eyes when the incorrectly attired neck of the waiter bent to allow the man to ogle Portia's lovely and generously displayed cleavage, though. Whilst perhaps contributing to his present predicament, these things where merely forerunners of his troubles, not the problem itself.

The first real hint of trouble had been the third thing Daz had not quite believed; the prices at The Salmon-Ella. He was sure that if they had the seafood platter he'd still be paying for it days later. Daz had believed, erroneously as it happened, that he could reason with the aforementioned waiter.

Daz politely excused himself from the company of the lovely Portia and sought conference with the man. He'd attempted to explain that his current funds were insufficient to pay for the meal and that he did not wish to disclose this to his companion. Daz was, he explained, completely willing and able to pay for the meal, if only part of the payment could be deferred until the following Friday. He had offered his watch to prove his good intentions. The waiter had not simply refused. That would have been embarrassing, but understandable. He had laughed; loudly and at length. Even that, Daz could have tolerated.

The waiter then proceeded to the table where the voluptuous Portia was seated and shared his mirth with her. Unfortunately, both for himself and the situation as a whole, his merriment had dimmed his powers of expression. In attempting to speak concisely, he referred to the delightful Miss Pinkley-Smyth as, 'a cheap date'.

Daz had thumped him one. Got him good and proper.

Correctly dressed waiters had promptly appeared and Daz had learnt that the less than appreciative recipient of his powerful upper-cut was not, as he had supposed, a waiter. He was in point of fact, the rightful owner and sole proprietor of The Salmon-Ella. Deciding that a prompt departure was better than valour, Daz left, taking dear Portia with him. He had returned her immediately to her father, the perplexed judge.

Daz had explained all. The judge had asked questions. Daz had answered them as fully and accurately as he felt was prudent.

"But the tie? Explain yourself man," Portia's Papa had demanded.

"Sir, it was knotted exactly the way that you yourself knot your ties."

"Impossible! Quite impossible!" blustered the judge.

"I assure you, sir," countered Daz.

"He's right, Daddy," Portia confirmed.

"But that's the way we did it at the dear old school. Only old boys wear… Did you perchance learn the name of this fraudulent waiter?"

"Yes, sir. Walter Walterson."

"Warty watery Walter? Blast the man. He was expelled for the most atrocious atrocities, most of them directed against me. You thumped him, did you say?"

"Yes, sir. Got him good and proper."

"Well done man! Splendid, splendid. Well, we can't have you and Portia eating at The Salmon-Ella. I'll ring my club, have them get you a table ready and put some champagne on ice." The judge then placed his mouth close to Daz's ear and whispered, "and I'll have them put it all on my tab."

Daz almost couldn't believe his luck, until the judge called out after his departing back.

"And you bring my daughter straight home, or it'll be you getting thumped good and proper!"

19. A Matter Of Routine

Philipa sighed. She was ready to take the kids swimming and as usual Grant was fussing. He checked opening times online, sorted the right coins for the parking meter and lockers. He'd already chosen where they'd eat afterwards and booked a table. It was a good choice of restaurant; Philipa could have a classy salad while the kids gorged on pepperoni pizza. It would be a fun day out and nothing was likely to go wrong, she should be grateful for her reliable husband and his meticulous planning. Should be.

Grant checked he had his credit card, that it was in date and he'd got the loyalty card for the petrol station in case he needed more fuel. Grant would never, ever, run out of petrol, but Philipa could easily run out of patience. She glanced out of the window as she counted to ten.

That man was hurrying by and, yet again, Philipa couldn't help wondering where he was going and what he'd do when he got there. Sometimes he was smartly dressed, sometimes casually attired. Often he wore a long, brown 'camel hair' coat. Usually he walked, or ran, to the garage block to collect his car, but sometimes he carried on towards the train station. Often he had a large, apparently heavy backpack on, sometimes just a small bag. He was never empty handed and Philipa took to thinking of him as Mr Camel because of the coat and baggage.

He always looked as though he were going somewhere spontaneously. Maybe even he didn't know quite where he was going, or what to expect on arrival? He always looked attractive too …as did Grant, she reminded herself. Grant's blond good looks were characterised by well planned neatness, whereas Mr Camel was darkly and romantically dishevelled.

The only reason Philipa was tempted to rush out after him was to discover where he was going. She was just curious. There was no need to follow Grant anywhere; if she wanted to know where he was she just looked in their diary at the careful notes he'd made. She could rely on Grant. Reliable was good; not dull, not really.

Grant had allowed for the road-works so Philipa's family arrived at the pool in plenty of time. Philipa managed to swim a fair few lengths before it got too busy. She hauled herself onto the side to watch for a while, getting back in later to encourage her youngest as he practised a new stroke.

When they left the sports centre, another family, very like Philipa's own were going in. She caught her breath as she noticed the father hurrying along behind. He carried a large bag and wore a long brown coat but it wasn't her Mr Camel. Hers? What was she thinking? He was nothing to do with her, probably hardly even knew she existed.

Grant was speaking, saying something about disappointment.

"What did you say, love?"

"They'll be disappointed, that family. They'll have less than twenty minutes in the pool arriving at this time, they should have checked."

The father wasn't so different from Mr Camel then. He wouldn't have checked before taking his family out.

"Maybe not. They might decide to go somewhere else instead, somewhere exciting and different."

"Perhaps" Grant agreed, but she guessed he was thinking, as she was, that there wasn't much scope for exciting and different with six and four-year olds in tow. Or was he thinking back to the days when he and Philipa had first started going out and they'd never planned a thing because all they'd cared about was being together?

At the restaurant, Grant and the kids ordered the same meal they always had. Philipa tried the special, even though it was described in Italian and she had no idea what she'd be getting.

"I'll ask the waitress to translate," Grant offered.

"No, don't," she snapped.

"But you might not like it."

"Good."

The special turned out to be seafood pasta, which was good because she'd never had that before. Admittedly she'd not had it because she didn't like squid, mussels and whatever those chewy orange bits were, but that wasn't the point.

Wisely, Grant didn't say anything, not even after Philipa pushed her half full plate away. Once the family got back home they put away their swimming things, made a drink and settled down to watch a film. Of course they did, that's what they always did on Saturdays. As she put the children to bed, at their usual time, Philipa gazed out the window. She didn't see Mr Camel coming home. Was he already back, or was he still out there, doing something unexpected?

On Sunday they did all the stuff they always did on Sundays and on Monday, they did what they always did on Mondays. Tuesday was the same. By Wednesday, Philipa wanted to scream at someone, anyone. She bit her tongue and tried to create just a tiny break in their routine.

"Would you like coffee?" she asked Grant at breakfast.

"No, tea please."

He always drank tea with his toast.

"I could make a pot of real coffee if you like."

"No thanks, love."

She made them both tea, just as usual.

"Not having coffee?" he asked her.

Of course, she should have done. Grant wasn't going to change, but that didn't mean she had to be stuck in his dull routines.

She took the children to school, as usual; washed up, loaded the washing machine, vacuumed, all just as usual. She cooked her lunch, but only ate half of it. She abandoned the remains on the kitchen table and went out, buttoning her coat as she strode down the road, just as she'd seen her handsome mystery man do. She got the bus into town intending to go shopping, even though a visit to the supermarket wasn't scheduled until Friday. She almost laughed at her excitement over her tiny spontaneous gesture. All she'd planned was to serve something other than the usual Wednesday menu of sausage, beans and mash for tea. Then she saw him; the man in the coat.

He seemed to have noticed her too, because he stopped in the middle of the shopping centre as though waiting for her. As she approached he smiled.

"Hello," Philipa whispered.

He held out a hand. "Hello."

Philipa couldn't think of anything to say, but luckily Tom, that was his name, wasn't phased by a chance encounter. He talked about the weather, asked what she was doing and offered her a lift home. She hadn't bought anything yet, but that didn't prevent her accepting. At home, she tidied up from her lunch, collected the children and ate sausages for tea when Grant got home, exactly on time.

Philipa didn't see Tom in the shopping centre on Friday, neither did she buy as much food as usual. Other than that everything went on exactly as it had before. Until Wednesday. Philipa went into town again and bumped into Tom. It might have been coincidence that he was in the same place at the same time two weeks running; it certainly wasn't his routine because he didn't have one. She was almost sure he was looking for her. When he found her, he offered a cup of coffee. Philipa accepted that and a cream cake, even though, or perhaps because, she didn't usually eat in the middle of the afternoon.

Tom was perfectly charming. He complimented her on her appearance and it felt like genuine appreciation, not something scheduled.

Grant never failed to say she looked nice whenever she'd had her hair done, bought a new outfit or when she emerged from the bathroom ready to go out on their birthdays or anniversary, but he just said what he always said.

Tom flirted a little and made her laugh with stories about his job. He was a freelance photographer and often called to take unusual pictures. He hinted there was room for an assistant occasionally. His life sounded fun, exciting and unplanned. When the bill was presented, Tom didn't have quite enough cash to pay. He rummaged through his wallet and things fell out. There was an expired video shop membership card, a discount voucher from a store which closed three months earlier, crumpled receipts and eventually the card he was searching for.

"Here, let me," Philipa said, putting down enough money

for her half of the bill.

Grant gave her a lift home and suggested meeting somewhere the following week.

"Oh, um …" Philipa mumbled. Bumping into a neighbour and having a coffee was one thing, arranging to meet an attractive man was something else.

"Just for a drink," he coaxed. His eyes promised something more, although exactly what she wasn't quite sure. It was probably the uncertainty that persuaded her to accept.

The following week wasn't like it normally was. Philipa and her family did just what they always did, but she didn't feel the same. Most of the time Philipa was excited. She was looking forward to meeting Tom again. She wondered where they'd go and what they'd talk about. Would he kiss her, ask her to come on an assignment? Sometimes she felt guilty as though she were actually having an affair. Doing that would be easy to organise. Grant never came back early, or rang up out of the blue. As long as she picked the children up from school and had the correct meal cooked on the right day, he wouldn't suspect a thing.

Philipa was so excited she arrived over half an hour early for their meeting. That's all it was, not a date or anything like that. She decided against ordering her usual cappuccino and chose an Americano. It wasn't very nice, but it was good to try something different, wasn't it?

The coffee shop door opened exactly at the time she'd arranged to meet Tom and Philipa put her hand up to wave at him. A boy she didn't know came in. For a moment she was confused, if she'd been meeting Grant, he'd have arrived exactly on time. She waited almost a quarter of an hour. If Grant had been that late, she'd have worried, but she wasn't waiting for her husband. Her organised, reliable husband was at work.

Tom didn't apologise for being late, he probably hadn't even realised he was. "Where would you like to go?" he asked.

"The butchers."

"I don't understand. I've got a couple of hours spare; I thought we'd go somewhere a bit more, er, interesting."

"I've run out of sausages, I need to get more for tea tonight."

Tom laughed. "Is that all? Don't worry, we'll call in somewhere so you can buy something for your husband's supper tonight."

"We could, but nowhere else does the same sausages we like."

"Well, have something else then."

"Good, idea." Philipa dropped the exact change for her coffee on the table and walked away from Tom. She thought he called after her, but she didn't make out his words and she didn't turn back or even slow her pace.

When Grant came in from work, he was greeted by Julio Iglesias on the stereo, a wife with a new hairstyle, his whole family dressed in yellow and red and the distinctive aromas of garlic and saffron wafting from the kitchen.

"What's happening?" he asked.

Philipa kissed him and said, "We're having a Spanish night."

"Er, OK. Right. Do I have time to change?"

He always got changed when he came from work. He never looked quite so puzzled though.

"Don't worry, love, I just fancied a change. We'll be back to sausages and mash next week."

He nodded and headed for the stairs.

Philipa did the finishing touches to the meal and poured wine for her and Grant. The children were given cranberry juice in wine glasses, so it looked almost as though they were all drinking the same. As usual, Grant walked into the dining room, exactly when the food was placed on the table. What wasn't so usual was the shrieks of laughter from the children as he entered.

She turned to see him wearing his frilly dress shirt, her black leggings and with her long red skirt draped over his shoulders.

"Ole!" he said."I am Juan, ze famous bullfighter. Do any young bulls dare to fight me?"

The children squealed and rushed towards him, pretending to charge. Grant dodged about for a while, waving her skirt like a matador's cape, before scooping up a giggling child under either arm. "I win and now I can claim my prize!" he declared.

"What is it, Daddy?"

"I don't know love. Mummy will give it to me later." He winked at Philipa. "I'm looking forward to a nice surprise."

That made two of them.

20. Celebrate Life

The letter-box crashes just as Mary finishes adding milk to her son's cereal. Distractedly she glances through the post. Half her mind is on whether the phone bill will be higher again and half is listening to the children's arguments about the contents of their lunch boxes.

There is a leaflet from the local church inviting her to join with them in celebrating her life. Mary drops it in the bin. She doesn't have time for that sort of nonsense. Another envelope has the name of the local health authority stamped on it with smudged red ink. Mary remembers her smear test of three weeks ago. This letter might be nothing to do with that of course. It could be a survey, or something. She will not speculate on the contents she tells herself firmly. She has three children to get ready for school, before she goes to work.

"No Stephanie, you may not swap the apple and carrot sticks for an extra chocolate muffin."

"But Mum, my friend Allison gets cakes and chocolate and crisps and coke. It's not fair."

"How many fillings do you have?"

"None, but …"

Her mother silences her. "And how many does Allison have?"

"Three."

"Do either of you like going to the dentist?"

"No."

"See; it is fair."

Eventually the children are ready. Their coats are on, their shoelaces tied and their bags slung over their shoulders. They should walk to school Mary realises, but it's easier and quicker to drive them. Stephanie and Gavin are dropped off together. They rush off to meet their friends without a backward glance. Ian, her youngest is less self-assured. She parks the car and walks with him to the door. Guiltily, as he reaches for her hand, she remembers he'd wanted to discuss something with her. At the time she was ironing her work uniform whilst keeping an eye on their tea. She said they'd talk about it later, but she hadn't found the time. She kisses him goodbye. She can still see him in her mirror, waving, as she drives away.

Mary arrives at work almost on time. She hates the drive. She shouts abuse at other drivers, using words she'd never use outside the car. Mary appears at the shift meeting, closing the poppers on her tunic and tying back her hair. She is pleased to see Angela this morning. They are not often on the same shift. The supervisor agrees they can take their break together.

Angela works on the next checkout, the supermarket is busy and they don't have a chance to chat. They grin at each other occasionally, but that's all the communication they manage. Sadly Mary is reminded of her marriage. She smiles at her husband over her children's head as he gulps down coffee before rushing out to catch the train. He doesn't get back until nearly eight, by then all they want to do is eat supper slumped in front of the TV.

During the coffee break Mary remembers her letter from

the hospital.

"What's wrong, chuck?" Angela asks, "You've gone awful white."

Mary passes her the letter.

"Oh poor you. I hate smear tests the first time round, its tough luck having to have it done again."

"What does it mean?"

"What it says. The results are unclear and they need to check again."

"It could be cancer."

"Well it could, if it is you'll soon find out and get treated. But it's not really likely now is it?"

Mary tries not to worry about something that might not happen, but occasionally she feels weepy. Sometimes she snaps at the children or Mike for no good reason. She knows concerns for her health are making her act out of character.

When she eventually confides in Mike he sounds almost relieved.

"I thought you were going to ask for a divorce."

"Why would you think that?"

"You haven't been happy lately and I know you went out a couple of times without mentioning it."

"You've been checking on me?"

"Ian mentioned Angela had collected him from school. I thought there would be a good reason, but was surprised that you didn't mention it. I never guessed it was for medical appointments."

"You could have asked me, taken an interest."

"Lately you seem to resent any kind of interest from me."

Mary feels guilty then. It's true; she has shut him out both emotionally and physically. No wonder he's confused. She explains her concerns. She asks if the insurance will pay someone to look after the children if she dies.

"Don't talk like that, you're not going to die. This is just a silly scare; we'll go out to celebrate once they give you the all clear."

"That won't be for a while yet." She hands him the latest hospital letter. It is an appointment to see a consultant next week.

"They did find something you see. It's in the early stages. The consultant can probably remove it completely. Apparently it's not a big procedure."

"Oh, love. How could I cope without you?"

"Untidily."

"That's for sure."

"You would cope though. And you'd know if I was haunting you. I'd be the first poltergeist who ever put things back in the cupboards."

They try to laugh at her joke.

"I don't really think I'll die, Mike. Only occasionally I think the worst could happen. But right now I just want to make the most of every minute. I want to celebrate being alive and having a good chance of staying that way."

On Friday Mike leaves work early. They walk together to collect the children from school. They play rounders in the park on the way home. Lots of other children and a few adults join them. Mary laughs a lot and no one has any idea which team wins. For supper they have home made pizza instead of the usual frozen one. With parental help Stephanie makes the dough and Gavin rolls it out. Everyone helps chop vegetables, herbs, cheese and ham. Each person has an individual pizza over-topped with their favourite ingredients. When they've eaten Mike explains as gently and honestly as he can that Mummy will be going into hospital for tests. She might have an operation. She should get better quickly, although it's possible that she'll need more treatment.

"Will you go with Mummy?"

"Yes we'll walk you to school and then I'll take mummy to hospital. If I'm not back in time Auntie Angela will collect you. OK?"

"Can we visit Mummy?"

"If she stays in hospital I'll take you every day."

"But you'll be at work. You're always at work until after bed time."

"I'll come back early and take you. I promise."

The whole family spend the weekend together. They walk through the local country park taking a picnic lunch. They use books from the library to try and identify the birds and wildflowers they see. On Sunday they have a huge traditional lunch. They sit together and talk whilst they eat. No one takes a tray to watch television or play computer games.

When Mary sees the consultant she learns that the abnormal cells are clearly visible and can be easily and completely removed with a loop excision.

"I can perform the procedure this morning if you wish. Did someone bring you in today?"

"Yes, my husband."

"Shall we tell him to come back in a couple of hours? You should be able to go home by then."

"You mean it will be over? I'll be OK?"

"Yes, you will feel uncomfortable for a couple of days and

should rest. Just follow the advice leaflet we give you. There should be no lasting effects."

The children are delighted to see their mother wrapped in a quilt, on the sofa surrounded with every pillow Mike could find. Mary clutches a hot water bottle and swallows painkillers. Physically she feels rotten, but emotionally she considers herself the luckiest woman in the world.

Mike insists on making a fuss of her for a while.

"But I'm fine really, I just have to avoid heavy lifting for the next month, so I'll need you to carry the hoover upstairs and unload the shopping. Apart from that I can do most things."

"I know, but work gave me time off to take care of you. I'd feel a fraud if I didn't. Besides I want to."

"OK, I agree. You can start by defrosting the freezer. No, actually bring me a cup of tea and a bowl of hot water first."

"Oh?"

"I'm going to soak my feet, when you've done the freezer you can give me a pedicure. I think I'll take this pampering lark seriously."

"Pedicure? I don't know how."

"Got the instructions right here." She waves her magazine at him, then shoos him out the room.

Over the next couple of days Mike completes the household tasks that Mary had been putting off for a while. He massages and moisturises all the body parts that she feels would benefit. They decide that Mary is well enough to go out. They do things they used to do, before children and work took up all their time. Looking round charity shops was something they'd done a lot of before. They used to get clothes for the fancy dress parties their student friends all threw. They'd looked hopefully among the trinkets hoping to spot something valuable. Of course, neither of them really knew what they were looking for, it had just been a game, some cheap entertainment.

Mike spotted a fondue set.

"Do you remember ours?"

"Oh yes, didn't we think we were smart?"

"We should get this, the kids would love it."

There was no instruction leaflet, so they looked through the selection of recipe books.

"Got one." Mary held up a book, 'Stylish dinner parties for modern couples on a budget'.

"What a mouthful."

"So are the recipes, nearly everything has Avocado in it. I'd forgotten how trendy that used to be."

"What about all those fancy gateaux and theme cakes. I liked them," Mike said.

"You like any kind of cake."

"Remember how we always had cake for tea, now we only have it on the kids' birthdays."

"Funny that, it's almost as if we need an excuse to treat ourselves."

Another book is spotted, 'Celebration Cakes.'

The children love the fondue, probably because their parents have made a chocolate one, with fruit and marshmallows to dip. When they spot the cookery books, Mary hears giggles and whispers. Aware of a family conspiracy she tries not to notice the shopping trip or the fact that she is being kept out of the kitchen the following day. She doesn't have to pretend surprise when she sees the cake.

"It's to celebrate you getting better, Mummy."

The cake is topped with marzipan figures representing the family. They are arranged on chocolate and surrounded by sugar flowers. Mary insists on taking a photograph before it is cut. The children stand round their masterpiece, proudly pointing to their own contributions.

"It might not look exactly like the picture in the book, but it should taste OK," Mike says.

It does.

When the children are in bed, Mary and Mike snuggle up on the sofa.

"It's been great to see a bit more of you lately, Mike. I'll miss you when you go back to your regular hours."

"I'll miss you too. And the kids. I hadn't realised how little I see of them. I want to see my wife and children everyday not just the weekends. I'm going to get try to get a job closer to home."

"Better get that book out again and I'll choose a cake for next week."

"Really, why?"

"I think we should celebrate our life."

21. Swept Away

Jamie ran along the coastal path ahead of Hilary.

"You not coming, Mum?" he called.

"There's someone else, down there," Hilary said. She knew she should have stayed away.

Jamie came back. Together they looked down. A man, and a boy about Jamie's age, were at the water's edge writing words in the sand and watching the tide erase them.

"But it's not their beach; it's ours," Jamie said.

The beach wasn't Hilary's, although she'd once felt it was.

Eight years ago when she and Jamie's father were on honeymoon it seemed their own private place. They'd written words of love in the sand and kissed until the tide came in. She guessed the tide had swept away the words before they'd got back to the hotel. That didn't matter; their love would last longer. It had; but not long enough. She didn't like to calculate how soon Tony's marriage vows had been swept away by the redheaded girl in the accounts department where he worked. Hilary been so lonely since then; no one seemed to understand how she felt.

She wouldn't have returned to the beach except she'd won a week away for a family of four in a competition advertised in the local paper. She'd hoped for a runner up prize of a half day in a health spa. She rang the organisers to say she wasn't a family of four. Half an hour later they called back.

"You can still take the holiday. We're going to contact the

runners up and if any of them are in the same situation we'll offer them your unused half of the prize. I imagine single parents are even more in need of a break than bigger families are."

"That's true," she'd agreed. Hilary did feel in need of a break away and Jamie would love a holiday by the sea. She accepted her prize.

Yesterday it had been cold and the beach was deserted. Jamie had been so happy running about after his kite, throwing a Frisbee and skimming stones. Hilary had enjoyed herself too. She thought she'd made the right decision in coming here. That was before she'd seen a man writing in the sand.

"Mum?" Jamie looked worried and she realised she'd been paying more attention to the past than to him.

"What love?"

"Is it their beach?"

"No, anyone can go there."

"Come on, then." He ran ahead again.

Jamie tried flying his kite, but it was difficult. The wind wasn't as strong as previously and both he and Hilary were unable to ignore the man and boy who continued their game of writing words and watching them disappear, laughing together as the sea washed away the letters.

Jamie's kite dropped down near the couple. He ran to retrieve it, then stood near them and called to Hilary.

"What are they doing, Mum?"

The other boy answered. "Making nasty things go away."

"How?" Jamie asked.

Hilary came close to Jamie. "Come on, love; leave them in peace." She held her hand to him and said sorry to the man.

"No problem." He smiled.

Hilary thought she recognised him. He frowned at her as though he too was trying to decide if he'd seen her before.

"I know you, I think?" he asked. "Did I see your picture in the paper?"

"I won a trip here, so you may have done."

Hilary remembered now; his picture had been next to hers as he'd been awarded half her prize.

"Then thank you," he said and offered his hand.

Hilary shook it and introduced herself and Jamie.

"I'm Mike and this is Danny."

"So how do you make bad things disappear?" Jamie asked.

"Easy," Mike said. "What don't you like?"

"Broccoli."

"Go on then, Dad," Danny urged.

Mike wrote the word in the sand, then they all stood back and watched the sea sweep it away. The boys both cheered.

"Anything else?" Danny asked.

"Mum crying," Jamie said.

"Jamie!" Hilary felt her face flush.

Mike wrote 'crying' and they watched it vanish.

"I've already done loneliness," Mike confessed.

"And it's gone?"

"For the rest of the week at least?" Mike gave a hopeful smile.

"I suppose the beach is big enough for all of us," Hilary said. She had done the right thing in coming back.

22. Are You Tough Enough?

I come in from school and head to my room.

"Jake, I want a word with you," Mum calls as I'm halfway up the stairs.

"I'll be there in a minute, Mum," I reply.

I wonder what she wants now. Maybe I've got time for a quick drag before I get my ears bent. Now where did I hide my cigarettes?

"Now, Jake."

She doesn't sound happy, but then she's often not happy with me. Always having a go or nagging about something. 'Do your homework', 'eat your veg' or 'brush your teeth.' Never stops she doesn't; treats me like a kid all the time. I'm not a kid. Next year I'll be old enough to join the Marines, well old enough to apply. They don't let you join until you've left school. She'll stop treating me like a kid then.

"Jake, are you coming down?"

Damn, I can't find the fags. I'd better go and see what she wants, then I can have a quiet smoke in peace.

Mum holds up my ciggies as I saunter into the kitchen. She reads from the pack.

"'Smoking kills,' now why do you suppose it says that?"

"To scare people?" I guess.

"But it doesn't scare you?"

"Nah, why would it?"

"So you think it's good for you?"

"Good for my image. Gotta look tough if you're going to be a Royal Marine."

"I imagine it takes more than the right look. Others things will be important, such as good health?"

She has a point. "Loads of people smoke and are fine, look at Granddad."

"That's supposed to cheer me up? You know your Granddad is ill?"

"Fuss over nothing he said, anyway he's old."

"Jake!"

"I didn't mean he's ready to die, you know I don't want that. I just meant it's not surprising that he's not healthy at his age."

"He's sixty-nine."

"Exactly."

Granddad's a great old bloke, or used to be, but like I said, he's old. He can hardly say five words now without that awful wheezing starting up. Still, he's been smoking for years without any trouble. I hardly smoke any; I can't afford enough to do me any harm, so I don't know what the fuss is about.

"Can I have them back now, Mum?" I ask pretty reasonably.

"No you can't," she yells back and crumbles my fags up.

"Hey, they were expensive."

"You will not smoke in my house and you won't be getting any more pocket money until I'm sure you won't waste it on cigarettes."

"That's not fair."

"Oh grow up, Jake."

We don't really talk for a bit. That gives me time to wonder why she's so against smoking. Normally I can get round her all right, but not this time. Maybe it's because of Granddad. It's a shame he's not feeling too clever. He used to tell me loads of stories about being in the Royal Marines. He used to carry me on his back, pretending I was his rucksack and we'd go yomping. He taught me some self defence stuff and survival training. All kinds of stuff. He doesn't show off his medals, except for Remembrance Day. He lets me help clean them then. I want to make him proud when I join up.

"Jake, can we talk?" Mum asks eventually.

"What about?" I try not to sound too bolshie as I come back into the kitchen.

"I've been thinking about what you said, about your image, joining the military all that sort of thing. Perhaps you're right, I don't understand and I am protective of you. You know it's just because I want the best for you, though, don't you?"

"Yeah."

She looks like she might cry or kiss me or something.

"Fancy a cup of tea?" I ask and start filling the kettle. I'm not great at all the soppy stuff.

"Maybe you should stay with your granddad for a while, he's a lot cooler than I am," Mum says.

"Granddad?"

I mean, sure he was something in his day, but not now.

"He must be, he understands about the marines, he could help with your training and he wouldn't give you a hard time about smoking as he does it himself. I know he's not young, but we all get older, even you."

Mum looks sad and tired. She's always done her best for me and I know she hates it when we fall out. So do I.

"Sure, Mum. I'll go to Granddad's for a while if you think it's a good idea."

She's all smiles now.

"He'll be pleased."

'Course, I should have thought, this isn't about me. Mum keeps telling me that not everything is about me. You'd think I'd have grasped that by now. Obviously, she's worried about Gramps and wants me to look after him for a bit. I can do that, then she'll see I'm responsible.

Living with Granddad isn't like being at home. It's more like being on exercise. Everything we eat is out of tins. We keep ourselves clean and the house tidy, but there's no polishing or arranging bunches of flowers. Granddad's as wheezy as ever and he keeps gobbing up loads of phlegm. The bins soon fill up with his disgusting tissues. I miss being at home.

He shows me some old photos, him in his RM uniform complete with green beret, some in ceremonial gear, some in camouflage clothing. With each one I get the full story, sometimes it all sounds a bit far fetched, until he comes across a whole bundle of medal presentation pictures.

There seems no end to the things he's done and the stories he has to tell. Lots of photographs aren't formal portraits, they're snaps of him and his mates. In everyone Gramps is smoking a roll up. Nearly always, the men are in uniform, often with their berets tucked into a belt loop and a smear of cam cream across their faces. They look so cool; I'm going to be just like that when I join.

"Proper hero you were," I tell him, but he doesn't think so.

"Just doing my job, lad."

"But you were brave."

"Not really. You get the training and when you're there," he gestures at the photos, "you just do what you have to."

"Do you ever see any of the others?"

"Yes, Jake and so will you; we're off to the pub tonight."

This is more like it, instead of being at home doing my homework with mum, I'm down the pub with Granddad's ex-service mates. He's obviously told them about me. I get introduced to everyone.

"This is Road Runner, we call him that because he runs marathons."

"What about you, Jake, ever considered trying it?" the ex Marine Sergeant asks me.

"No, I couldn't do that."

"Thought you wanted to join The Corps, you can't become a Royal Marine if you're not fit."

"I'll start training and become as fit as you."

"I'd like to think you'd be a damn sight fitter than a chap of sixty-nine."

"Sixty-nine." I can't help repeating it like an idiot. This man is the same age as my Granddad but nowhere near as old, if you know what I mean.

It's great being treated like a grown up for a change. I have to drink coke of course, but that's the only difference. They don't look guilty if they swear, or keep the jokes clean for my benefit. No one says a word whenever I go outside with Granddad and a couple of the others for a smoke. Well, no one except Road Runner. He tells me gramps is a fool to waste his cash on tobacco. He gets a pen and writes figures on a beer mat.

"What's a packet cost, at least a fiver now I bet?"

Although I know it's far more, I agree.

"I bet the silly old duffer smokes the whole lot in a day?"

"More than one," I tell him.

"Two then, that's seventy quid a week."

Actually, Gramps often starts on a third, but I keep quiet. I'm beginning to see why he buys tinned soup and baked beans rather than steaks and takeaways.

"So, say there's fifty weeks in a year, just to make the maths easy, comes out at three and a half grand."

Hmm, maybe there are some advantages to not smoking.

Walking home is a slow business. Granddad's wheezing is worse than ever and he seems tired. I talk about Road Runner.

"What's his secret do you think?" I ask.

"No secret, he looks after himself that's all. Didn't you notice the difference between us?"

I don't know what he means, sure Road Runner was fitter, but he was doing the same as Gramps. They even drank the same brand of beer.

I'm still thinking about Road Runner the following morning. Granddad points him out in one of the medal presentations. I don't know if he got as many as Gramps and I'm not going to ask, but he's certainly something to live up to.

"There's still one of my ex Marine buddies that I'm in touch with, who you haven't met. He got more medals n' me and Road Runner put together. I thought we could visit him today."

It's hard to believe that the shrivelled body under the

oxygen mask was once a hero. He's got something called Chronic Obstructive Pulmonary Disease. It doesn't sound or look pleasant. The bloke seems pleased we're there. Gramps chatters away to him, I can't understand the whispered responses. Granddad's friend is soon tired and we get up to leave.

A man in a white coat is coming in as we go out. He stops to talk to us.

"So have you quit smoking yet?" he asks gramps.

"I've cut down a bit, but it's not easy, Doc."

Why doesn't Gramps stand up to this bloke?

The doctor turns to me, "Perhaps you'll talk some sense into him. If you don't want your grandfather to end up like that chap in there, then get him to quit smoking."

I don't want to think that the doctor could be right. Granddad looks upset and I can't think of anything to say. We just go.

"I can't give up lad, I'm too weak," Granddad says when we stop outside so he can get his breath back.

"You're not weak."

"Yes I am, I know what the fags do, but I can't give them up. The addiction is stronger than I am. I know it's made me ill, but I don't want you to end up like him."

He pointed to the ward where his dying friend lay.

"Or like me. I want you to be another Road Runner."

"Gramps, you know what you said about your medals? How it wasn't just you who won them, but the whole troupe? That you were stronger together?"

"I do. It's true. The camaraderie and support help you achieve things you'd think were impossible."

"Do you think that together we could learn to be stronger than a packet of fags?"

He looks at me for a long time. "Maybe."

We don't go straight back to his house. We stop at the health centre on the way and make an appointment for the 'stop smoking' clinic. Gramps and I will make each other proud. Mum'll be happy too.

23. Splitting Up

"Yaz, is this your phone or mine?" Harry asks, holding the sleek device above his head.

I pat my jacket pocket and locate my identical phone. "It's yours."

"Maybe one of us should put a sticker on ours, so we don't keep getting them mixed up?"

"Good plan."

Telling his property from mine hasn't always been so simple, nor so free of pain.

Eleven years ago it had been agony. Back then I'd been faced with three heaps of belongings. Mine, his, ours. I'd just learned there was to be no more ours, which is why I was sorting through all the stuff. Tears dripped onto things which were once ours and which I must either claim as my own or give up as his.

"I need space, Yaz," Harry had said.

"I'll give you space," I promised.

I really would have tried. If we could have been together at home I wouldn't need to be with him all week too. We'd travel together, any alternative arrangement would just be silly, but we could go our separate ways as soon as we got out the car. I could arrange for my desk not to be so close to his, I'd suggested. I wouldn't spend lunch breaks with him. At least not all of them. We have friends in common so of course we'd sometimes end up eating in the same group.

He had to be with me at night though, I told him. It was comforting when I woke to hear him next to me. If he was awake we chatted and if he was asleep I just listened to him breathing. The deep, hypnotic rhythm sent me back to sleep. At least it did. He didn't want to sleep next to me any more. How would I get used to that after seven years of him always being there?

"We have different interests," he said.

"Not really," I argued.

We liked to go to the same places, eat the same things, watch the same things on TV. Our taste in music was the same, and our sense of humour, and we both liked to count the seconds between thunder and lightning.

OK so I'm not as keen on football as Harry and I couldn't imagine him suddenly developing a passion for ballet, but what did that matter? If we spent a little time with our own friends, pursuing activities that didn't involve the other one, surely that would have given him the space he needed.

"You just don't get it, do you?" he asked.

"No, Harry. I don't."

How could I? All my happy memories involved Harry. Every Christmas and birthday he'd been there, celebrating alongside me. Every holiday had been spent with him. It was Harry who'd squeezed my hand before take off and who'd raced me down the beach the minute we'd checked into the hotel and dumped our bags. Sometimes he'd let me win (usually when he guessed the water might be cold!)

All my sad memories involved Harry too. It was his shoulder I'd cried on when my little cat got ran over. It was him who'd broken my heart when he said he was moving out.

"It's you who doesn't get it, Harry."

Why didn't he? Why couldn't he see we were supposed to be together always. Yaz and Harry, Harry and Yaz. We were a couple, a set, a pair. Everyone thought so. Almost no one thought of us separately. No one except Harry, apparently. We looked right together. Were right together.

"I'm nothing without you," I'd wailed.

He'd left, slamming the door in a childish gesture.

I'd flicked through our photograph album. Probably not the best thing to do, but I couldn't help it. As I looked at the photo of me clinging behind him on his bike I could almost feel the wind rushing by. I'd felt that I'd never travelled so fast in my life.

There were pictures of us in fancy dress. Two halves of a make-believe pony, a king and queen from a chessboard, two zombies. I put the album on his pile. Maybe looking at it would make him see sense.

Next I picked up a t-shirt. His. I'd worn it once and he hadn't been happy. Neither of us had worn it again. Thinking back, my pulling on his t-shirt might have been what pushed him away. I hadn't asked to borrow it, just assumed he wouldn't mind. No, not even that. I'd thought that what was his was mine and always would be. I'd been wrong. His things weren't mine and now neither was he.

My quiet tears turned to noisy sobs. Even so I heard a sound as I drew in a long, shuddering breath. A quiet tap on the bedroom door. My heart missed a beat as I looked up. Not Harry, Mum.

"Oh, Yaz love," she'd whispered. Mum sank down beside me and pulled me into her arms. She rocked me like a baby until I was calm enough to speak.

"Why, Mum? Why is Harry moving out?"

"You're both seven now and it's time for you and that twin brother of yours to have separate rooms."

His had been right next to mine, and I'd gone in there often. Just as he'd spent time in what had been ours, but was then just mine. Sometimes though he shut his door, a sign he wanted time to himself; something I too soon came to appreciate.

"Yaz, you OK?" Harry asks, bringing me back to the present.

"Sure. I was just thinking… about our old photo album."

"That's spooky because last night I scanned some of the pictures onto the computer. Want to see?" He hands me his phone and I see the two of us dressed as zombies.

"Even death couldn't have kept us apart," he says.

It's true. We're going off to different universities soon, and one day we'll have our own homes and families but we'll always be a pair in some ways. Harry and Yaz. Yaz and Harry.

24. Big Loser

I almost walked into a lamp post when I realised who it was that Del reminded me of. You'd be surprised too if you were a twenty something girl who'd just recognised yourself in her retired male neighbour who sported the craziest moustache outside of Cuba. I don't mean we look alike; I'm as pale as he is dark. He's a good foot taller and several stones lighter. Yeah, you've got it – he's fit and I'm fat.

So what had caused me to see myself in Del? It certainly wasn't his clothes. If Del is ever tempted to wear floral prints and lacy blouses, which I doubt, he doesn't do it in public. Somehow, I get the feeling that he always looks smart, even reading his paper on Sunday mornings. What then? His expression? Attitude? Something like that reminded me of myself this morning.

I'd stepped onto the scales and saw I'd lost half a stone. That was pretty good I thought. The reflection of my naked body didn't seem quite so horrific. When I got dressed, I was sure the waistband of my skirt felt just a little less tight. My grapefruit and black tea breakfast tasted just a little sweeter. Walking to the bus stop for work wasn't quite such hard work.

No one noticed. Not even Tanya. As she was the one who talked me into starting this diet in the first place, you'd have thought she'd have been the first to appreciate the difference. She did congratulate me for sticking with the plan when she joined me for a coffee break and saw I was snacking on celery instead of the caramel filled chocolate bars which, until a month ago, had been my regular break-time treat.

"Sticking to the plan and sticking to the schedule," I informed her. "I've lost half a stone."

Tanya squealed and hugged me.

"Brilliant, Becky! Didn't I tell you you could do it?"

"No one's noticed though," I moaned.

"You have. It's you who is important. I saw you walking in this morning and you had a real spring in your step. I think you look a bit healthier too. All that fresh fruit and veg is doing your skin good."

I grinned. I'd thought the same thing.

"Do I look any slimmer?" I asked hopefully.

"Well, it's hard to say …"

"Which means no."

"It'll soon be much more obvious," she encouraged.

"A whole month of depriving myself and I don't look any better. What's the point?"

"The point," she reminded me, "is that since you split up with that rotten ex boyfriend more than a year ago, you've put on half a stone a month. As you were, well you said you weren't …"

"Not anything approaching skinny to start with?"

"Yeah, that. Since putting on more weight you've been wrecking your health, confidence, your whole life to be honest, Becky."

"I know I was and thanks to your encouragement and advice I'm now eating sensibly, taking control again and changing all that."

"Exactly. If you hadn't started the diet, you'd be half a

stone heavier now, not lighter, so in a way you're a whole stone better off."

"I suppose."

I looked into my plastic container, hoping the celery would have magically changed into something more interesting. It hadn't.

"Fancy a piece?" I said as I offered the box to Tanya.

Her expression made me laugh.

"Suppose not. I wouldn't if I was you."

If Tanya were to lose as much weight as I'm trying to, she'd be a black hole. I can't even complain she's scrawny. She's slim; pretty too. If I didn't owe her my sanity, I'd probably hate her. You see, I was depressed when I first met her. It was Tanya who persuaded me to talk about Mark and helped me to start getting over him. She recommended me for this job and when she thought I was ready, she stood over me while I booked an appointment with the dietician.

"Sorry," I said. "Moan over. How are you? What have you been doing?"

After listening to her describe a typical family weekend – caring for a four year old, toddler twins, her husband and their Springer Spaniel puppy and keeping the house and allotment tidy I could understand how she kept her figure so trim. Poor woman probably didn't get much time to eat. I pushed the thought of exercise away. Deep down, I knew it would be a good idea for me to do some but I didn't want to acknowledge the fact. I'm not co-ordinated, have no rhythm and get red faced and sweaty just walking up the stairs. With my lack of confidence, proving to myself I was a complete failure at something else just wasn't an option.

On the bus home, I decided to work out a bit more of the

weight loss schedule. The dietician had suggested half a stone a month. I'd done that once, I could do it again – right? So in a month's time I'd have lost a stone. A month after that… I'd still be obese. By the end of the year I'd still be overweight. By the next summer my weight might, just possibly, be OK. I'd still be me though. Still be alone.

I got straight off the bus and strode over to the cake shop. Even that short distance when taken at a brisk pace had me breathing heavily. It was bad enough waddling into a cake shop, without wheezing over the assistant so I waited outside to get my breath back. That gave me time to admire the trays of pastries, muffins and eclairs in the window. Which should I have? I could select an entire lardy cake and carry it home to be eaten warm from the oven and washed down with sweet milky tea. That might put back on all weight I'd lost over the past month in a single evening. I found I wasn't quite ready to give up to that extent. Maybe something smaller really would be better? Meringues aren't too fattening if you don't count the cream filling and chocolate drizzled across them. I might not count the cream, but I'd certainly eat it. A fruit tart then? Fruit is healthy. The buttery pastry base and gooey custard layer less so.

Then I saw Del. I'd have been in that shop for certain if I hadn't seen him. Or if I'd thought I could have avoided him seeing me. Stupidly, I'd told Del about my diet.

He invited me round for tea and a chat sometimes and once I started the diet, I'd had to make sure he didn't tempt me with biscuits. He'd been really impressed and I just couldn't buy a bag of doughnuts or whatever with him watching. I waved and hurried home. Then, like a lightbulb pinging on over my head, I understood his expression.

He'd been looking around, just as I'd done that morning,

when I was hoping I'd see someone who'd notice my weight loss. Del wanted to be noticed, he wanted to talk. Something good had happened and he thought the joy of it would be obvious to everyone around him. Probably it would have been obvious to me if I'd not been wallowing in self pity. Del had been hinting for a while that he had some kind of happy secret plan. He must have achieved whatever it was. Like me, he was on his own. He's a lovely bloke, he deserved someone to share his happiness with. Maybe I wouldn't be anyone's first choice, but even in my misery, I hoped I'd be better than no one.

Narrowly missing the lamp post, I turned round and walked back up the street. Del was coming towards me. He was grinning so hard his moustache looked like it was crawling up the sides of his generously proportioned nose. Then I noticed the enormous great cigar in his hand. Del doesn't smoke. He used to, he told me. When I'd told him about my diet, he said he guessed it would be hard and would take a long time, but he knew it would be worth it. I couldn't believe that after I'd deprived myself of the sugary pastries and chewy cookies I so desperately needed that I was now watching him give in and start smoking.

"What's that?" I snapped.

"Victory cigar, but don't you worry, I'm not going to light it." He was apparently too happy to notice my sharp tone.

"Good, but what victory?"

"Aha, not long now and you'll find out! Got that camera ready?"

He'd asked me before about sending pictures abroad. He wanted to know how quickly it could be done. I'd explained that with a digital camera and the internet, I could send a photo anywhere in the world within minutes of taking it.

He'd been delighted and got me to promise I'd do exactly that for him one day. Seemed that day had come.

"What is it, Del?" I asked.

"Well, you remember I told you how I'd given up smoking?"

"Yes, you stopped when your son was born because you wanted to watch him grow up, not have him watch you coughing up your lungs," I said in almost his exact words.

"That's true, but it wasn't the whole reason. The day before I discovered he was expected, I'd seen … well, let's just say it was something I hoped to buy. I couldn't afford it and to raise a child. I didn't begrudge that, not at all. When he was eighteen someone offered me a cigar. Can't remember who it was now, but Tony heard me explain how I'd given up smoking because of him. He got all choked up about it and as a joke, I told him what else I'd given up for him."

"That's such a lovely story," I said. "I hope he appreciated your sacrifices?"

"He did, still does. When he got his first wage packet, he gave me the price of a cigar and said he'd keep on doing it until I could afford …"

"What? Come on, Dell. He stuck to it, didn't he? You're going to buy whatever it is?"

"Already done it!" The moustache was trying to climb into his ears. "Go get your camera."

I did as he asked. While in the house, I booted up my computer, so I'd be ready to send the picture if he really did want it to go quickly. When I went back round to his house, Del was chatting to a man who was climbing out of a really cool looking car. Vintage I reckoned, and American. The paint work was immaculate and an incredible turquoise colour. That and the chrome gleamed in a way that made me hope my camera would do it justice. Del shook hands with the driver who walked away, carrying a number plate under his arm, just like people do when they deliver new cars.

"You've bought a car?" I asked rather stupidly.

"I have. Now take that picture and we'll send it off to Tony."

Del posed in his car, the cigar clutched awkwardly in his hand and the moustache doing a Mexican wave. I took his picture, making sure enough of the car showed for his son to be able to identify it. We rushed round to my place, dashed up the stairs and I sent off the email. I was out of breath and red faced when he replaced Tony's business card into his wallet and took out a photograph of the man. I was almost glad of my red face then as it hid my blush. Although I'd realised Del was Tony's dad, when he moved in, I'd never admitted it. I'd been to school with Tony and had a huge crush on him before I'd started dating Mark. The man had been gorgeous then and it looked like he'd actually improved since.

"Do you know him?" Del asked almost innocently. "He said he used to know a girl by the same name."

"We were at school together. What have you told him about me?"

"What a lovely girl you are. How you took it hard when you split with your boyfriend, but you're picking up the pieces now."

"Why did you tell him that?"

"He's just had a nasty divorce. I thought it'd be nice for him to know someone in the same position, sort of."

"But he doesn't know me."

"No, but he will when he moves back here in two months time."

"Oh."

Two months? I'd have lost a stone and a half by then. That's if I continued as I was. I would continue, that was for sure. It must have been hard for Del to give up smoking, but he'd done it for his son. It had taken Tony years to save for his dad's car, but eventually he'd got what he wanted. I could lose my extra weight. Yes, it would be partly to justify the faith Del and Tanya had that I could stick to the diet and partly in the hope that Tony might notice me, but mostly it'd be for myself.

"Fancy coming for a drive with me, in my new Cadillac?" Del offered.

"I'd love to, but only one way. I'll walk back, the exercise will do me good."

I knew the spring that had been in my step this morning and in Del's this afternoon would be there as I walked. I hoped we'd never lose that.

25 Home Port

There was quite a wind as we waited along the sea wall. I was glad of it as that would explain my tears, though why I'd be worried I couldn't say. Nobody would be looking at me. Those wives and sons, mothers and sweethearts would all be looking away from shore. And they wouldn't notice my tears anyway, or if they did they'd take them for joy or relief that the ship, all its crew safe, was pulling into harbour.

A little boy tugged at my sleeve.

I smiled down at him.

"Daddy be home soon."

"Leave the lady alone, Danny," a woman, presumably his mother, told him.

Danny? I looked a him properly. The boy looked like his mother though his hair was darker. Just the colour my son Daniel's had been when he was that age. Could Daniel have a son? Of course he could and one the age of this boy. This child could be my grandson and I wouldn't know.

How could I have been so stupid and for so long? I'd been a navy wife once, just like the woman next to me. Not a very good one; she's better I'm sure. I'd never brought Daniel to watch his father's ship come and go, though I knew it was what they'd both wanted. We'd said our goodbyes at home and waited there for Matthew's return. I did write and he phoned me but I behaved as though I thought he were away on holiday. I moaned all the time about being stuck at home with the baby while he was off visiting interesting places.

Rarely had I spent time with other naval families and I wouldn't step inside the dockyard. In short I made things difficult for my husband and I didn't really know why.

I tried to blame the navy when he died. He drove home straight off deployment. It was late, he was tired. Other wives fetched their husbands, or stayed with them in the married block that night. Daniel would have loved that; to watch his dad's ship come in, go into the dockyard to hug him and help carry his kit into barracks. We should have done that. Or at the very least when he phoned to say he was back but tired I shouldn't have whined they were later than expected and that dinner was spoiling. I should have done anything but make him drive home.

The navy, his friends, did what they could for me. It wasn't much, I wouldn't allow it. I was angry with them, with myself and even with my son. Daniel had idolised his father. Never moaned when he left, was overjoyed when he returned. He understood his father's work, his life, far more than I ever did. He wouldn't throw out the uniform or burn the photos or wipe away every memory of the sailor he'd loved.

"Danny, I said to leave her be."

I saw the child was again trying to attract my attention. Trying to talk to me just as Daniel had.

"It's OK, I don't mind," I assured her. The woman, who for all I know was my daughter-in-law.

The boy tugged again and said. "Have you come to see the ship?"

"Yes."

"Daddy's ship?"

"That one out there," I pointed. "Is that your daddy's

ship?"

"Yes. It's HMS Underland. That right, Mummy?"

"Close enough," she said as she grinned at me.

"Are you waiting for my Daddy too?"

"My son," I said. I could hardly have told him I didn't know, could I?

"He on the ship?"

"Yes."

"What does he do?"

I didn't know the answer to that either. When at fifteen Daniel had come home with recruitment literature from the navy I'd ripped it up and forbidden him from ever mentioning the subject. He didn't, not until he was eighteen and told me he'd been accepted to join. That was the last time we'd spoken. Rather than spend every precious moment with him before he'd started his training I'd kicked him out.

He wrote and invited me to his passing in parade. I didn't reply, didn't go. He rang to tell me when he was joining his first ship. I hung up. How could I have been so stupid? The navy had been an important part of his father's life; a part I hadn't known. It was important to my son too and as a result I no longer knew him at all.

Then one day I'd seen Daniel's picture in the local paper with the headline 'Sailor lost at Sea'. I'd collapsed in the high street.

I don't remember much of what happened but people came to my aid and I ended up in a church drinking hot sweet tea and learning it wasn't Daniel who'd been lost. He had been part of the search and rescue party when a yacht had run into difficulties somewhere off the coast of Africa. I talked then to the lady minister and later someone my doctor referred me too. I came to see my hatred of the navy was really fear. I'd been scared of losing my husband and then my son and had lost them both anyway. One was lost forever, but perhaps not both.

"My daddy's a sailor," little Danny informed me.

"Yes my son is too."

"What's his name?"

"Daniel," I said. Watching the mother's face I added, "Daniel McCaffrey." She didn't react with anything more than a smile.

"Daddy's called Ichard."

Danny was not my grandson then. Perhaps I didn't have one yet. Actually I was sure I didn't. Daniel would have written to tell me. I'd torn up all his letters, but not until after I'd read them. He'd never turned his back on me the way I had him.

The ship was by then close enough for Danny to begin yelling to his dad. Soon it was close enough for his mother to wave. I waved too and all the sailors waved back. My son was waving at me, I was almost sure I could identify him though it was unlikely he'd recognise me. He wouldn't be looking for me of course. I wasn't sure he'd have waved if he'd known I was there. I thought he would though. Hoped I'd not left it too late.

When the ship had passed by, and people had waved and taken photographs until it turned the corner into the dockyard out of sight, the sea wall began to empty of people.

"Go see Daddy now?" Danny asked.

"Not quite yet. He's still working, remember?"

"They have to park the ship first and do work and then we see him?"

Little Danny understood in a way I'd never been willing to.

"You doing now?" Danny asked me.

Another of his questions for which I had no answer. I wanted to see Daniel but realised it was impossible. I had no idea where to go or when and couldn't get into the dockyard without a pass anyway.

"There's a nice little café just over there," Danny's mother gestured.

"Have cake?" Danny asked.

"No, we'll wait in the car. We've got the flask and biscuits."

I invited them to join me in the cafe. "My treat."

"Yes please," Danny answered before his mother could begin her polite refusal. "Cake please."

His mother shrugged and shook her head, but she grinned again when I said how pleased I was to have their company.

Danny busied himself with a gooey slice of chocolate fudge cake. He did try using the fork but took such large pieces he needed to hold it on with his fingers and even then smeared much of it on his face.

His mother took over the questioning. "My Richard has a mate they call Mac's Cafe, would that be your son?"

Asking unanswerable questions seemed to be a family trait. "I don't know," I admitted.

Danny offered a laden fork to his mother. After she'd nibbled at the offered chunk of sticky chocolateyness he refilled his fork and waved it in my direction. I was so reminded of my husband sharing his treats with Daniel and I that I leaned forward to take a pretend mouthful. Danny helpfully lifted the fork higher, coating my nose in rich icing. I laughed as I wiped it away, then cried as it hit me again that memories were all I had left of my son.

"They're both chefs," Danny's mother prompted once I'd finished with the tissue. "Richard and his friend."

"I don't know what his job is, but Matthew was a chef too, so it's likely Daniel is." Then I told her a little about Daniel and his father.

"Mummy, why lady crying?"

"Because she misses her son just like we miss Daddy when he's away."

Danny held my hand. "Do crying now. Smile when you see him. That right, Mummy?"

"That's right, love."

I knew then her Richard had not seen her tears, that Danny hadn't seen the loneliness possibly even anger that she must have sometimes felt. She coped somehow. She'd taught Danny to cope. I could learn to do the same for my son, if he'd let me.

"Would you mind Danny for me, while I go to the toilet?"

"Yes of course."

I'm not entirely sure that buying him a milkshake and second piece of cake was what she had in mind, but that's what I did. It wasn't until I added coffee for his mother to the order I realised I was trying to keep them with me and thereby possibly keeping them away from Richard. His wife looked happy enough when I told her more refreshments were coming though.

"Danny'll probably be too excited to eat later anyway."

We talked for quite some time after that. Or rather we answered Danny's questions as best we could. I'd forgotten just how inquisitive they are at that age.

"It's time to go meet Daddy," she said eventually.

Danny held my hand as well as his mothers as we walked toward the dockyard. It didn't seem to occur to them I wouldn't be going along too and I was reluctant to leave their company and return home alone.

"I don't have a pass or anything to get in," I admitted as we drew nearer the dockyard.

"It's OK, Richard is meeting us just outside."

Soon we saw a group of sailors waiting outside the gate. One moved toward us waving.

"Daddeeeee!"

Nothing either of us woman could have done would have stopped him running to his father. My companion followed her son only a little more slowly. Richard hugged his son tight, lifted the boy onto his shoulders and then hugged his wife.

My eyes filled with tears, blotting the view of a reunion unlike any I'd had with my husband. But that I could have had. Should have had.

Around me other sailors greeted loved ones or jumped into cars and taxis. I just stayed put until one stopped in front of me.

"You came to meet my ship?"

"Daniel?"

He's grown I swear. Or I've shrunk. Whatever it was my boy was gone forever, replaced by a man with his father's shy smile.

"Yes I've come at last. I hope I'm not too late?"

He picked me up and hugged me.

Later I told him I'd waved when the ship came in. "It

looked like you waved back at me."

"I always do, Mum."

Later, much later, I learned my husband too had been called Mac's Café by his friends and I wondered if he'd ever waved to no one as his ship came into port. I would never know, but I promised myself our son would never have to again.

Thank you for reading this book. I hope you enjoyed it. If you did, I'd really appreciate it if you could leave a short review on Amazon and/or Goodreads.

To learn more about my writing life, hear about new releases and get a free exclusive ebook, sign up to my newsletter – subscribepage.io/ItLSNa or you can find the link on my website patsycollins.co.uk

More books by Patsy Collins

Novels

Firestarter
Escape To The Country
A Year And A Day
Paint Me A Picture
Leave Nothing But Footprints
Acting Like A Killer

Little Mallow cosy mystery series

Disguised Murder and Community Spirit in Little Mallow
Dependable Friends and Deceitful Neighbours
in Little Mallow
Deadly Words and Innocent Gossip in Little Mallow

Non-fiction

From Story Idea To Reader
(co-written with Rosemary J. Kind)

A Year Of Ideas:
365 sets of writing prompts and exercises

Short story collections

Over The Garden Fence
Up The Garden Path
Through The Garden Gate
In The Garden Air
Beyond The Garden Wall

No Family Secrets
Can't Choose Your Family
Family Feeling
Happy Families

All That Love Stuff
With Love And Kisses
Lots Of Love
Love Is The Answer

Slightly Spooky Stories I
Slightly Spooky Stories II
Slightly Spooky Stories III
Slightly Spooky Stories IV
Slightly Spooky Stories V

Just A Job
Perfect Timing
A Way With Words
Dressed To Impress
Coffee & Cake
Not A Drop To Drink
Making A Move
Criminal Intent
Crime In Mind
Days To Remember
A Clean Bill Of Health
Your Good Health

Non-fiction

From Story Idea To Reader
(co-written with Rosemary J. Kind)

A Year Of Ideas:
365 sets of writing prompts and exercises